THE GUNS OF
SACRED HEART

THE GUNS OF
SACRED HEART

Clifford Blair

Walker and Company
New York

First published in the United States of America in 1991
by Walker Publishing Company, Inc.

Published simultaneously in Canada by Thomas Allen & Son
Canada, Limited, Markham, Ontario

Library of Congress Cataloging-in-Publication Data

Blair, Clifford.
The guns of sacred heart / Clifford Blair.
p. cm.
ISBN 0-8027-4123-1
I. Title.
PS3552.L3462G86   1991
813'.54—dc20   91-15978
CIP

Printed in the United States of America

2   4   6   8   10   9   7   5   3   1

To my wife, Alma,
whose love and presence
are a constant support
and encouragement to me

THE GUNS OF
SACRED HEART

CHAPTER 1

THE cold and the snow seemed to cut through to the marrow of his bones. Tom Langston hunched his shoulders and tried to still the brittle chattering of his teeth. Astride his horse, he pulled his worn mackinaw close around him. His Stetson was jammed tightly down on his head, and his bandanna covered his ears and his face to just below his eyes. It was not enough. The cold still penetrated, numbing his legs even through his long johns, jeans, and heavy leather chaps. He was beginning to think there could never be enough clothing to keep him warm on this frigid night.

His wiry pinto mustang lurched awkwardly and went knee-deep in a treacherous drift. Normally surefooted as a puma, the mustang was not used to heavy snow clogging the draws and gullies of these rugged wooded hills. Tom was not used to it, either. Winters in central Oklahoma Territory were known for their fierce wind-driven cold, not for snowy blizzards that piled up two feet of snow in a little over twenty-four hours.

And it was just his luck to be caught out in it, he mused darkly. His fruitless search for the strayed Bar D Ranch heifers had brought him into these hills. For most of the day, riding in the falling snow, he had crisscrossed the region, seeking the missing cattle. He had expected the snow to stop, not to continue to pile up and drift beneath the shifting winds as the hours passed.

By the time dusk was falling he realized that he could not make it back through the snow to the ranch and the warmth and security of the bunkhouse. He also realized that he might not survive camping out in the low temperatures. It was then he remembered the deserted cabin nestled in the hills to the east. He did not know the origins of the cabin. Likely it had been built and finally abandoned by disheartened home-steaders. Or maybe it had served as a haven for outlaws prior to the opening of the Territory for settlement. But he knew it offered him refuge.

He headed east as night turned the terrain into an eerie, treacherous fantasyland of white slopes and skeletal trees shrouded by a veil of wind-driven snow. Even more bitter cold seemed to descend with the darkness.

With the wind behind it, the snow penetrated every open-ing in his clothing. It worked its way eventually to naked flesh and touched him with icy fingers. The exposed part of his face had long since lost any feeling. The rest of his body was growing numb. The leather work gloves he wore provided little insulation to his hands. His fingers were clumsy as he manipulated the reins.

A tendril of fear stirred in him as he wondered if he had missed the cabin in the snowy gloom. Landmarks were all but nonexistent now. He was forging ahead on instinct and a prayer.

A vagary of the wind teased his nostrils with a familiar scent. Wood smoke. He lifted his head and peered into the pale gloom. Had he imagined it? Then the mustang tossed his head and snorted eagerly. He too had caught the smell and knew that it meant sanctuary.

"That's it, Paint," Tom tried to encourage the animal. His mouth wouldn't form the words correctly beneath his ban-danna, and he doubted the mustang heard him. But Paint surged ahead with renewed vigor.

There. Tom thought he caught a glimpse of light. He blinked against the snowflakes blurring his vision. He could see a faint gleam through the intervening snow and trees. He urged the mustang ahead.

As he neared, he made out the boxish shape of the cabin and the lean-to adjacent to it. Yellow light shone through a piece of oilskin stretched tight across the window. The wind wafted the scent of woodsmoke to him again. Plainly some other wayfarers had already taken refuge in the cabin and they had a fire going, he thought gratefully.

Paint needed no prodding. He plowed eagerly through the snow for the last few yards. Tom dismounted and led the mustang into the shelter of the lean-to. He could make out the dim shapes of two other horses tethered inside. With fumbling fingers, Tom unsaddled Paint and rubbed him down with hurried strokes. There was much snorting and pawing of feet as the other horses tested the newcomer's scent.

He was careful to tie Paint far enough from the other horses so there would be no fighting. The lean-to provided adequate shelter for the animals. Tom knew the mustang had drunk earlier in the day from a rapidly freezing stream, so he would not need water again that night. Worrying about feed could wait for the morrow.

He shouldered his saddle and forced himself back out into the wind. He staggered to the cabin door and pounded on it with a gloved fist. "Hello the house!"

For a moment only the whining wind answered. Then "Who's there?" came a gruff muffled voice.

It was a rude response to a stranger under the circumstances, Tom thought with irritation. He resisted the impulse to try the door. It was probably barred. He pulled the bandanna down from his face. The cold clawed at his naked flesh. "I need shelter!" He shifted the heavy burden of the saddle on his shoulder.

"How many are you?" the voice demanded.

"Just me!" Tom reached angrily for the door.

It swung open before he touched it. He recoiled slightly. A sawed-off shotgun menaced him from a foot away. It was in the grip of a partially visible man standing to one side of the door. "Slow and easy, pardner. Keep your hands where I can see them."

"Let me in, for pete's sake!" Tom shouldered his way through the doorway into the warmth and light of the cabin. His reluctant host stepped warily back.

Tom heeled the door shut and lowered his saddle carefully. He eyed the man behind the shotgun. He saw a tall bearded stranger with age starting to show in his lean features and graying hair. Pain had pulled his face tight. A crude blood-stained bandage could be seen on his shoulder through his torn shirt. The shotgun was a Greener. Despite his wound he held it with competent familiarity. A revolver was sheathed on a gun belt that was as functional and nondescript as his shapeless clothes. A U.S. marshal's badge was pinned lopsidedly to the breast of his shirt.

A second man was crouched by the dilapidated frame of a massive old bed in a dim corner of the room. Metal gleamed briefly at the man's wrist as he shifted. Tom realized that the fellow was handcuffed to the sagging bed frame. His hunched shape bulked large in the shadows.

"Who are you, boy?" The sternness of the lawman's tone might have been mostly a result of pain. His eyes were as gray and hard as slate, just the same.

"Tom Langston." Tom repressed a shiver and clamped his chattering teeth tight together.

"What are you doing out in this weather?"

"I ride for the Bar D Ranch," Tom explained. He couldn't blame the wounded marshal for being leery of strangers. "I was looking for strays and got trapped when the snow kept coming down. I knew about this cabin. I figured I'd sit the storm out here."

The slate eyes appraised him. They lingered on the Colt slung at his waist. After a moment the lawman backed carefully to a sagging cot and settled into it with an involuntary grunt of pain. From his half-reclining position he could command the entire cabin with the Greener.

Tom forced himself to look away from those ominous barrels and survey the cabin's interior. Beyond the marshal's cot, the bed frame, a cookstove, a table, and two rickety chairs, there were only fragments of furniture. A battered potbellied stove provided the heat. Some prior wayfarer, or perhaps the cabin's original occupants, had left a supply of firewood inside. Two lanterns gave shifting illumination.

"I'm Breck Stever," the lawman announced. "U.S. marshal out of Guthrie. I've got a prisoner here I'm taking in for trial."

Tom nodded. The situation into which he had stumbled was obvious. "I won't get in your way." He had to admire the marshal's grit. He was clearly not willing to let his wound keep him from performing his duty.

"I can't afford to be looking out for civilians with this man in my custody," Stever said flatly.

"My pa taught me how to look out for myself just fine." Tom's teeth had stopped chattering.

"That may be, but I don't know you from Adam. You could be in cahoots with him." He jerked his head toward the prisoner.

The handcuffed man spoke for the first time. "Aw, shoot, he's just some sorry cowdog, Stever. Can't you see that?"

Tom turned his glance to him. Sardonic black eyes studied him in return. The prisoner was a big man, with a broad face and black, stubbly whiskers. He carried some extra weight, but he didn't look soft.

"That's Ned Tayback," Stever said. "Maybe you've heard of him."

Tom glanced at the prisoner again in surprise. "I've heard."

Tayback shook his head ruefully. "The rumors do get around."

And, for certain, the rumors about this man had spread clear across the Territory. Ned Tayback was notorious. As reputed head of a wild gang of outlaws, Tayback was credited with crimes ranging from murder to horse theft to bank robbery. Tom had had his doubts that it was possible for one man to have committed all the crimes for which Tayback was blamed. Now, confronted with this big, easygoing fellow, he wondered just how many of the tales and rumors were really true.

"Don't let him fool you." Stever might've read his mind. "He's dangerous and sneaky as a starving lobo. He don't look the type, but he's prone to carry a hideout gun. It wasn't easy taking him. And his gang might be on the prowl looking for him. One of them already put a slug through my shoulder." He grimaced with pain.

"It was an accident, Marshal, I keep telling you," Tayback protested. "My boys ain't killers. Neither am I."

"The record says different," Stever rasped.

"That's just old women talking!"

Rumors or not, the marshal's position was a rugged one. "Maybe you need an extra gun backing you," Tom suggested to him.

The marshal nodded at Tom's holstered .45. "Can you use that?"

"I'm no gunhand, but my pa taught me a few things."

"Your pa again, huh?" Stever said skeptically. But the offer of assistance seemed to have balanced some obscure scales in Tom's favor. Stever finally lowered the shotgun. Tom felt the tension drain out of his shoulders.

"Well, I can't hardly turn you back out in a norther like this," Stever conceded. "You're welcome to stay, but you need to keep your distance from me and my prisoner."

"My pleasure." Tom hesitated. "Want me to take a look at that shoulder?"

Stever's lips thinned. "I said you keep your distance. I'll tend my own hurts."

Tom shrugged. "Whatever you say."

Tayback snorted with amusement. "Make yourself to home, cowdog. *Mi casa, su casa.*"

"*Gracias,*" Tom said dryly.

The outlaw laughed. "You and me'll get along, cowdog."

He rattled his cuffs meaningfully and grinned at Stever. "You and me could get along too, Marshal, if you'd give it half a chance."

"We're getting along just fine, as far as I'm concerned," Stever retorted coldly. "Remember, I can take you in dead or alive, either way. Dead just means fewer problems for me. And nobody's going to ask any questions about how you died."

Tayback shrugged with seeming unconcern. He turned his black eyes on Tom and winked as if they shared a private joke.

Tom looked away. He felt a growing respect for Stever. What the marshal had said was true. Many manhunters—bounty men and lawmen alike—would've felt no qualms about shooting Tayback down in cold blood in order to bring him in. And there would be only praise for the man who brought in Ned Tayback, no matter what the condition of the outlaw. It spoke high of Stever that, even wounded, he had chosen to try to take Tayback alive.

Tom moved to stand closer to the potbellied stove. He extended his gloved hands toward its welcome heat. He was still not ready to shuck his mackinaw or his Stetson. The cold had gnawed too deep into his bones to be quickly dispelled.

"It's a bearcat out there." Stever had lost some of his surliness. Now that he was settled in the cot, his wound seemed to be paining him less. "Never seen anything like it in these parts. Now, up north—Nebraska, the Dakotas—that's a different story. But this beats all for the Territory."

"You've been up north?" Tom asked.

Stever nodded. "I spent some time up there before I got assigned here. Yourself?"

Tom shook his head. "Family's from down Texas way. We don't see much weather like this down there."

"Who'd you say you ride for?"

The question sounded casual, but Tom knew Stever was double-checking his story. The marshal's complete trust would not be easily won. Tom peeled off his leather gloves and pocketed them in the mackinaw before he answered. "The Bar D. It's west of here. The Dayler family owns it. They run a thousand or so head of cattle and usually have a good string of riders working for them."

Stever nodded knowingly. "Old man Dayler still running things?"

"Yep."

"Still mean as the dickens?"

Tom met his slate gaze steadily. "Must be a different fellow. Old Jeremiah Dayler is as kind and God-fearing of a man as you'd ever hope to meet. He gave each of us hands a standing offer to stake us if we ever want to start a place of our own hereabouts."

Stever grunted. "My mistake. You been riding for him long?"

"Couple of years now." Tom wondered if Stever knew Jeremiah Dayler at all, or if he had been running some kind of bluff.

"I'm kind of out of my stomping grounds this far from Guthrie." Stever shifted as if to ease his wound. "Any towns hereabouts I can take my prisoner to when this lets up? I'll telegraph for a couple of deputies to come ride shotgun with me."

No U.S. marshal as competent as Stever appeared would be that ignorant of the towns in his jurisdiction, Tom knew. Guthrie, the territorial capital, wasn't that far to the northwest. Stever was still testing him. "Konowa's east of here," he answered. "Then there's the Sacred Heart Mission over the hills a few miles."

"Sacred Heart Mission?" Stever echoed. "What's that?" His question sounded genuine.

"It's a Catholic school for Indian girls. I doubt they'd have a telegraph."

"A girls school out here? I knew there was a mission of some sort, but I didn't know it was a girls school."

Tom sensed Stever's surprise was real. "I don't know much about it, myself," he admitted. "Just that it's there."

"You a churchgoing man, Marshal?" Tayback interjected.

Stever shot him a scathing look. "I'll attend your funeral," he gritted.

Tom indicated the grinning outlaw. "How'd you catch him?"

Stever was slow to look away from his prisoner. "God's own luck, I guess," he admitted. "I'd been trailing him and his gang after a stage holdup they pulled back near Guthrie. I wasn't hoping to do any more than locate their hideout so I could bring in a big force to take them. Well, I located the hideout all right, and while I was scouting it, I saw old Ned himself here ride out all by his lonesome. So I just naturally stayed on his backtrail to see where he was headed. Seems he has a little mixed-blood girlfriend he keeps in a cabin close to his hideout, and he was going to visit her. I just kind of waited until the time was right, then moved in and got the drop on him before he could hardly look over his shoulder and see me coming."

"But my boys almost caught you napping," Tayback boasted.

"Three of them just riding in spotted me with him," Stever elaborated. "They threw some lead before I could get us clear. One of them got lucky." He jerked his chin toward his wounded shoulder.

Tom resisted the urge to offer again to check the wound; he still hadn't won enough of Stever's trust for the marshal to let himself be put at Tom's mercy. He shrugged out of his mackinaw, which was growing damp from the melting snow on it. He hung it on a convenient nail, then undid his chaps from his legs. He draped them over his saddle. Now that some of the chill had left him, he realized that the cabin's interior still had an edge of coldness to it. Raw wind whistled between chinks in its aging log walls.

"You think his men are on your trail?" he asked Stever.

Tayback snorted.

"Maybe so," Stever said ruefully. "We lost that first bunch. They backed off when I downed one of them. But I expect they might've gone back to get help. Of course, the snow has probably slowed them down or stopped them altogether. For sure, it's covered our tracks."

"Oh, they'll come looking right enough," Tayback said. There was something ugly in his voice that hadn't been there before.

Tom guessed Stever was understating the entire tale of his pursuit and capture of the outlaw. To have tracked Tayback and his men, scouted their camp, and then to have apprehended Tayback single-handedly and shot his way clear— that was the stuff of legends. Despite his easygoing manner, Tayback must've been humiliated by his capture.

Tom used a dry rag from one of his saddlebags to wipe his chaps and saddle. After this soaking the saddle would eventually need to be oiled. He checked the Winchester in its sheath. He was conscious of Stever appraising him as he examined the rifle. The weapon would have to be cleaned.

"Wouldn't want to toss that pretty piece over here to me, would you, cowdog?" Tayback inquired. His voice had regained its earlier jocularity.

Tom ignored him. He shifted his saddle, then eased himself down with his back against it and his rifle close at hand. He was careful to place himself so the big outlaw's bulk was not outside his range of vision. He stretched his legs out luxuriously toward the stove, absorbing its heat with pleasure. He would never be warm enough again, he decided, but this was a start.

It was beginning to look like he would be stuck here with the lawman and his prisoner for some time. He had no idea how much longer the blizzard would last. And, even when it passed, the two feet and more of snow it had dumped on these rugged hills would make travel an ordeal.

He felt the first faint gnawings of hunger in his gut. He

disregarded them. He had some sparse provisions in his saddlebags suitable for a couple of days on the range. They might have to last awhile. He didn't know what in the way of provisions, if any, Stever had. He could get a mite hungrier before this was over, he figured darkly. For now, he was thankful to have found this refuge.

The warmth from the stove settled over him. Stever did not seem disposed to carry their conversation further. Even Tayback had fallen silent. Drowsiness pulled at Tom's eyelids.

From outside, over the rush of the wind, came the faint whinny of a horse. Tom's eyes snapped open. The sound had not come from the animals in the lean-to. His hand closed reflexively on the Winchester. He turned his head and met the challenging gaze of the lawman's slate eyes.

CHAPTER 2

"IT ain't mine," Tom told Stever. "I put him in the shed with yours."

Stever heaved himself up from the cot. He cast a glance at his prisoner. Tom saw that the outlaw's broad features were lit up expectantly. But there was puzzlement there as well.

Stever crossed to the door and stood to one side of it. He held the Greener ready in both hands. Only the grayness lining his face showed what the effort cost him. Tom rose smoothly to his feet, Winchester in one hand. Stever shot him a sharp look.

"Relax. I'm on your side." Tom moved to the other side of the door so that they bracketed it. He kept the Winchester's barrel angled upward. He could feel the wind probing through the cracks and crevices of the log wall. There was no back door. The oilskin stretched taut over the only window prevented any view out front.

Tom thought he caught the ghost of a despairing cry on the wind. He looked at Stever. The marshal was going to wait, just as he had waited when it had been Tom outside. The plaintive cry seemed to echo in Tom's mind, drawing him to its source.

"Cover me!" he snapped. With one hand he lifted the bar from the door. The wind shoved it open with a frigid blast. He stepped out into the teeth of the storm.

"Wait, you blasted fool!" The rest of Stever's protest was torn away.

Tom had forgotten his mackinaw. The cold clamped on him like a giant's fist. Thirty feet away he could make out the drooping shape of a horse with a rider sagging in the saddle.

12

With high, swinging steps, he forced his way through the drifted snow toward the rider.

"Help me, please." The words came to him faintly. He felt a stunned bewilderment. The plea confirmed what he had already sensed, but hadn't believed, hearing the earlier cry. It was a female voice. The rider was a woman.

As he reached the horse's side, she sagged still further in the saddle, then slid limply from it. He caught her awkwardly, the Winchester still gripped in one hand. He made a staggering turn back toward the cabin. Stever had emerged. He stood braced to one side of the door, swinging the Greener in short arcs to cover the perimeter. The wind plucked at his beard. His lips were parted in a snarl against the cold.

Tom plowed back through the snow, trying to use the same footholes he had made in reaching the rider. His burden made it hard. She was dead weight in his trembling arms. Stever barely glanced at him as he lurched past the lawman into the refuge of the cabin. He sank gratefully to his knees and tried to lower the woman gently to the floor.

"Cover me, and I'll get the horse!" Stever ordered sharply from behind him.

Tom tried to utter a protest. The marshal was in no shape to face the cold. But Tom's face was too numb for him to speak. Stever went plunging after the horse. Tom staggered to the door to cover him. The horse had scented the presence of the other horses in the lean-to. It had made a shambling start in that direction. Stever caught its reins without trouble. Leaning against the cruel pressure of the wind, he led the animal on toward the structure. Tom surveyed the snowy gloom. He squinted his eyes against the blowing snow, marveling at Stever's tenacity. He wondered if his numbed hands would even be able to fire the Winchester if the need arose.

In moments Stever reappeared, stumbling past Tom into the cabin. Tom backed inside in his wake. He used his shoulder to bull the door shut, and Stever fumbled the bar back into its brackets. Both of them were panting. Stever pushed himself away from the door, staring down at the prone figure on the floor.

"By the saints," he managed. "It's a woman!"

From his corner Tayback looked in silent astonishment.

Tom nodded. He set his rifle aside and moved to stand over her. "Help me get her closer to the stove."

Between them they shifted her near the potbellied stove. Tom's body felt drained. His limbs seemed as weak as a child's. Clumsily he knelt beside her.

A woolen scarf was wrapped around her head. Only her closed eyes were visible. As gently as he could, Tom unwrapped the scarf. A slender elfin face was revealed. Her blond hair was pulled economically back and done up behind her head. Her small mouth was open slightly as she breathed. The fair skin around her eyes showed the redness of burgeoning frostbite. Tremors began to rack her body.

Tom removed her coat and looked about for some sort of warm cover. The coat would soon be soaked through as the snow melted in the cabin's heat and would only increase her chill.

Stever appeared to read his thoughts. "Here." He produced a long heavy coat. "This has had a chance to dry out." He seemed earnestly concerned about her welfare, his wound for the moment disregarded.

She wore a light dress jacket and divided riding skirt, still reasonably dry. Tom spread Stever's coat over her as the lawman hovered. Tom cast him a curious glance.

"She looks some like my daughter, the last time I seen her," Stever offered gruffly. "Her ma died, and she's in school back East. I don't see her so often."

Tom expected some comment from Tayback, but the outlaw remained silent. Stever continued to stare broodingly down at the girl.

"You better get off your feet," Tom told him.

Stever ignored him.

"Then you might get some coffee ready for her when she comes around, if you're up to it," Tom suggested.

Stever grunted assent and turned toward the cookstove. His shoulders were beginning to sag with the weight of his wound. At some point he had set the Greener aside. Tom spotted it leaning against the wall close at hand.

Tom started to tuck the coat in around her. She stirred at his touch, and he pulled his hands back. Her eyelids fluttered, then blinked open to reveal bright china blue eyes. They widened in confusion.

"It's all right," Tom said hastily. "You're safe. You made it to the cabin. We've got you inside."

Some of the confusion faded. Tom found himself wanting to continue staring into her eyes. He drew away from her slightly.

She wet her lips. "Thank you," she stammered.

Tom knew from his own experience that her face was still too cold to allow her to speak with ease. "Hush," he told her gently. "Just keep still for a few minutes and we'll have some coffee for you."

He was conscious of Stever at the cookstove, dividing his attention between the coffeepot and their conversation. Apparently the lawman had already had some coffee brewed.

For a few moments she complied with his advice to lie still. Her intense turquoise eyes gazed steadily up at him. "I remember seeing the cabin," she said then, in a firmer voice. "I thought I must be imagining it. That's all I remember." She shook her head in mute wonder. "It really is a miracle. I was praying for one, and God gave it to me."

"We heard you call out," Tom explained. "You fainted just as I reached you."

She sat up, hugging Stever's long coat about her, and turned her head to survey the cabin. Tom saw her stiffen as she took in Tayback shackled in his corner. The outlaw smiled. "Howdy, miss," he drawled.

"He can't hurt you." Tom started to touch her shoulder

reassuringly, but stopped himself. "He's a prisoner of Marshal Stever over there. I'm Tom Langston."

"Pleased to meet you," she said with automatic politeness. "I'm Sharon Easton."

"What in thunder are you doing out in this norther, girl?" Stever had left the stove and come to tower over the pair of them. His gruff tone failed to completely hide his concern.

Sharon looked up at him. Her eyes widened. "You're hurt!"

"Forget it," Stever growled. "It's nothing."

She hesitated as if about to say more. But the storminess of Stever's expression seemed to dissuade her. "Please help me up," she requested softly instead.

Tom rose and offered his arm to assist her. She had to cling to it for a moment with one hand to catch her balance once she was on her feet. She shifted the coat around until it was over her shoulders. She was not quite as tall as Tom's chin. One-handed, Stever swung a chair around for her. She sank gratefully into it.

"I'm sorry." She managed a wan smile of apology to them both. Then she turned to Stever and said, "I was trying to reach the mission."

"You were headed for Sacred Heart?" Tom asked in surprise.

"That's right. I was due there yesterday, but the train was delayed. When I finally reached Konowa, I decided to rent a horse and come ahead on my own rather than wait for a messenger to be sent to the mission and then have them send someone to get me." She dropped her eyes. "I know it was foolish, but I didn't want to be any later than I already was. I didn't think I'd have any trouble finding it, even with the snow starting. But the snow just kept getting worse and worse." She broke off. A shudder that was as much from remembered fear as from the cold raced over her.

"You have business at the mission?" Stever pressed tactlessly.

"Yes," she answered, nodding. She looked up at him. "I'm going to be a teacher there."

"You're a nun?" Stever blurted.

"Oh, no." A quick blush suffused her youthful features. "They've started a new program of hiring laypersons as teachers. I'm the first." She lifted her head with unconscious pride.

Stever grunted noncommittally. Tom found himself smiling for no good reason. She looked up at him, then quickly dropped her eyes.

"Are you a deputy?" she asked.

Tom shook his head. "Just a cowhand. I got caught out in this like you, and came here looking for shelter. The marshal and his prisoner were already here."

She moved her head as if to turn and look at Tayback, but stopped.

"Are you feeling warmer now, Miss Easton?" Stever's voice was still gruff, but he seemed to be trying to make amends for his earlier bluntness.

"Oh, yes, much warmer. Thank you." She flashed him a quick smile. "And, please, both of you, call me Sharon. After all, you did save my life."

"I better check on that coffee," Stever muttered. He started to turn away. Tom saw him sway slightly. He wished the lawman would stop acting like a loco fool and get off his feet.

Sharon must've seen his momentary weakness as well. "No, I'll do it," she exclaimed. She rose quickly and took a step toward the stove. In midstride, she faltered.

"Here, don't fall." Stever reached to support her with both hands, then it was he who suddenly gave a strangled gasp and went pale as the snow. His legs folded. Tom managed to catch his sagging form. The marshal's exertions had carried their toll at last.

"Let me help." Sharon had recovered herself.

Tom felt her arms take part of Stever's weight. He was

extremely aware of her nearness. "On the cot," he grunted awkwardly.

Together they maneuvered him there. Sharon knelt on the floor at Stever's side. After a moment she looked up at Tom. Her face was still pale, but determination had sharpened her features.

"He's bleeding," she reported. "I've got to stop it."

Tom nodded. Leaving Sharon to her ministrations, he collected the Greener and eyed Tayback.

The outlaw bared his teeth roguishly. "Let me loose and I'll give you a hand with the marshal."

"Thanks," Tom responded dryly.

"No fooling," Tayback persisted. "I'm a fair hand tending to stove up horses and other critters like lawmen."

"I'll bet you are."

Taybuck chuckled.

Tom turned away. As he did, he thought a trick of the lantern light made the outlaw's eyes shrink and harden into shiny black stones. He looked sharply back at the big man. Tayback showed him all his teeth in that same easygoing grin. His eyes were just eyes. Tom shook his head and crossed to where Sharon still knelt by Stever's side.

The marshal was in a bad way. Handsful of snow finally stopped the flow of blood. Sharon removed the old bandage and bound the ugly wound with strips of a blanket. They tried to make the patient comfortable on the cot near the stove and its heat. Throughout the rough procedures Stever remained only semiconscious.

"He needs a doctor," Sharon said at last. Frustration was evident in her tone. "What can we do?"

"Come morning, we'll see how things look," Tom replied. It wasn't really any sort of an answer at all, he thought grimly. He was grateful when she didn't press the matter.

Tom put the Greener and his gear well out of Tayback's reach. The man seemed affable, but he was still a notorious outlaw. Tom checked the handcuffs securing him to the bedframe.

Tayback watched without expression. "It's mighty tight," he complained.

"It's a hard life," Tom drawled.

Tayback straightened himself and pressed his shoulders back against the wall. He appraised Tom shrewdly. "You look like a sensible man."

Tom shrugged. "My pa always said it was an awful sin for a man not to use the common sense the good Lord gave him."

Tayback chuckled agreeably. "You can use it now."

"How's that?" Tom asked skeptically.

"You can be smart, turn me loose, and let me go my way. No hard feelings. You take these cuffs off, and I call us even. Maybe I'll even be on the owing end to you."

"You're a mighty generous man."

"You bet I am," Tayback agreed seriously. "The hillfolks know me and my boys. They'll tell you that if a man treats me right, I'll do the same by him. Now, come on." He shifted about awkwardly. "Get these cuffs off."

Tom dug his teeth into his lower lip. He didn't answer.

Tayback stared up at him in bafflement. "Well, what're you waiting on, boy? Get me loose."

Slowly Tom shook his head. "I don't think so."

Tayback frowned curiously. "Why the devil not?" he demanded. "You think I'd hurt the little lady? Not a chance. I'm a regular gentleman. I told you—turn me loose and I'm owing to you. I'll ride out without another word. Won't even finish my business with the marshal."

Tom glanced at Stever, then turned his eyes again on Tayback. "Is that a fact?"

"You're buying into a game of trouble, if you're not careful, cowdog," Tayback insisted. "What choices do you have? You can't hold me, not when my boys come looking. And they'll come, you better believe. You're stuck here with a wounded marshal and a schoolmarm. What do you think you'll do when my boys do come?"

"I don't know just yet."

"There won't be nothing you can do, except get yourself and the marshal and the schoolmarm hurt without no cause. Think on that. You hang onto me, and all it'll bring you is a load of grief."

Tom chewed at his lip. "And probably a lot of heartache in the bargain," he added. He watched Sharon kneeling at Stever's side. Her shoulders were stiff with tension. He said to Tayback, "What proof do I have that you'd be willing to just ride out of here?"

"You got my word, boy!"

"Your word," Tom repeated.

"That's right! Now shake a leg. Just unlock these cuffs, and it's over." Triumph rode Tayback's voice.

Slowly Tom shook his head. "Reckon I can't do that, Tayback."

"Why not?" Tayback burst out.

"Well, for one thing, I don't think your word's worth an ounce of fool's gold."

"Well, what in thunder are you planning to do with me?"

Tom drew a deep breath. "I figure I'll see that you go back to stand trial."

"You're plumb crazy! You'll never live to see me in front of a judge. What makes you think you need to be worried about whether or not I stand trial, anyway?"

"Well," Tom answered thoughtfully. "I don't know if all the stories about you are true. But there must be something to them, since there's so many of them. And the way I see it, is that if I was to let you go, then I'd be at least partly to blame for whatever you did to add to those stories before you got corralled again."

"Why, you fool! Sounds to me like you ought to be the schoolmarm."

Tom glanced over at Sharon. Her shoulders had relaxed. "I reckon she does just fine," he opined quietly.

Tayback shook his head mournfully. "I swear, cowdog, you don't have none of that common sense."

Tom left him. Sharon looked over her shoulder at him as he went back to her. There was an almost relieved glow to her pretty features that had not been there earlier. Stever, Tom saw, was beginning to show signs of regaining consciousness.

Tom hunkered beside her. "Get some rest," he advised. "I'll look to him."

"No, that's okay." Ever so briefly, her eyes flicked to Tayback. "I couldn't help overhearing you talking," she confessed. "For a minute I was afraid you'd do what he asked."

"You mean turn him loose?"

"Yes."

"And you didn't want me to?"

"Oh, you mustn't turn an outlaw loose!" Her eyes were fixed intently on his face, and she lowered her voice as she continued. "Besides, I don't think we could take his word that he would just leave."

"Don't worry about him. He can't do nothing shackled up the way he is."

"But we still need to be sure one of us stays awake all the time to watch him, don't we?" she whispered.

Tom nodded grudgingly.

"You go on and rest, then," she ordered with soft firmness. "I'll watch him and tend to the marshal. You can take over closer to morning."

Tiredness was weighing on him like a burden of stones. Her suggestion was a good one. If they were to spend very long here, then they would have to establish a routine to ensure that Tayback was not left unguarded for any big piece of time. But some preparations needed to be made first.

"Can you use this?" He showed her the shotgun. The Greener, he figured, was a better weapon for her than a handgun or a rifle. In the confines of the cabin it would be darn near impossible to miss with it.

"I think so," she answered his question.

Briefly he demonstrated its operation. She nodded her understanding. "If he acts dangerous, point it and fire," he finished his instructions loudly enough for Tayback to overhear.

"I have three older brothers," she said. "Back home, when I was little, they used to drag me hunting with them as a joke. I learned how to use a shotgun. I finally got so good that they stopped taking me because I was showing them up." Her blue eyes shone with the memory.

"Where's home?" Tom asked.

"Kansas."

Tom took Stever's revolver and put it with his own gear. He settled himself against his saddle, his Winchester close at hand. "You didn't want to stay in Kansas and teach?" he probed.

"Not when I learned about the position with Sacred Heart," she told him earnestly.

It was pleasant chatting with her in the cozy warmth of the cabin, Tom mused. "It's a school for Indian girls, isn't it?"

"That's right. The government provides the funding. They have a wonderful program." Sharon sank gracefully to the floor and tucked her legs under her. She made an appealing image in the lantern light. "The Indians need to be educated in English if they're going to have any chance at all now that we've taken the last of their lands from them."

Tom knew she was referring to the series of land runs and allotments by which the United States government had systematically stripped the Indian tribes of the territorial lands that had once been promised to them. Yielding to growing public demand, Congress had gradually opened the whole of the Oklahoma Territory for settlement. Tom had already heard talk of statehood for the Territory. He didn't know if he liked the idea or not.

"Educating the Indians to our ways is a big order," he commented.

"I know," she assured him. "But we owe them at least that much after the way we've treated them. And it's important to them, and to the rest of the country as well. They can contribute so much if they're only allowed to do so." She had leaned toward him as she spoke. Her eyes were aglow with the depth of her sincerity.

Drowsiness was settling over Tom. He felt a dim envy of her dedication to her cause. He had no commitment of his own beyond a vague desire to one day have his own place with a small herd of good cattle. It wasn't much of a dream, he admitted to himself.

He thought he saw her mouth move in a faint tender smile before sleep pulled his eyes shut.

"Tom." Her whispered voice and soft touch awakened him. "I can't stay awake any longer. Can you take over now?"

He forced the grogginess out of his mind and took stock. Morning was not many hours off. Tayback snored in his corner. Stever showed little change beyond a slight flush to his pallid features. Tom frowned as he looked down at the lawman.

"It's like he's unconscious rather than asleep," Sharon said softly. Her face was drawn with tension and fatigue. She had more than pulled her weight of the guard duty, Tom realized.

He agreed with her analysis. He wasn't sure the symptoms were good signs. He wished for a doctor, or, at the very least, someone with medical skills beyond his own crude cow-trail variety.

"Go and get some rest," he told Sharon.

She hesitated, looking at Stever. Tom could see her eyelids drooping over her dim blue eyes. She gave a little moan of frustration and turned away. She curled up in a blanket against Tom's saddle. He added some wood to the potbellied stove. Their supply was getting low, he noted grimly; they would soon need more.

He became aware that Sharon was watching him silently from her position by the saddle. He forced a smile he hoped was reassuring. "Go to sleep," he urged gently.

"Okay." She studied him a moment longer. "Thank you," she whispered. Her eyes closed. In just a matter of moments her breathing became deep and regular.

Tom did a slow turn of the cabin. As if sensing Tom's presence, Tayback stirred as he drew near. The outlaw stared blearily up at the younger man. "How's the marshal?" he grunted.

Tom shrugged.

"He's worse, ain't he?" Tayback guessed. When Tom didn't answer, he went on, "Now, what about it? You've had a chance to sleep on it. How about turning me loose?"

"I think I'd have trouble sleeping again if I did."

The temperature in the cabin felt a shade warmer, he noticed. And the wind did not seem to be howling quite as loudly. He peeked past the oilskin through the window. The cold knifed at him, but the curtain of falling snow was not as thick as it had been earlier. Maybe the storm was dying at last.

He examined Stever more closely. The wound did not appear to be bleeding. No fresh blood showed on the makeshift bandage. Stever's flesh was warm—too warm? Tom wondered. Maybe it was only the higher temperature in the cabin now that the wind had died some. Tom could detect no reaction to his cursory examination. Stever was as limp and unresponsive as a straw scarecrow.

Tom positioned himself in a chair near Stever so that the cabin's other two occupants were clearly visible to him. Sharon slept peacefully. He had to fight the desire to stare for long moments at her sleeping face. Tayback began to snore again.

More than once before daylight, Tom almost dozed. Toward dawn, Stever's groan brought him sharply alert. He rose and studied the wounded man. Stever shifted about. It was the first movement Tom had seen him make since his watch had begun. The lawman's face was deeply flushed. Sweat beaded his forehead. Tom pressed the tips of his fingers against Stever's neck. His flesh was hot to the touch. It was not from the cabin's warmth, Tom knew now. Stever had a high fever, and that meant his wound was infected.

Stever groaned again, more loudly this time. He half turned onto one side, then flopped limply back.

"What is it?" Sharon's voice came from behind Tom. Her eyes were still drowsy. She clambered to her feet, shedding her blanket, and came to Tom's side. Her face paled as she saw Stever. Immediately she knelt beside him.

"He's feverish! We need some snow to cool him off."

"I'll get it." Tom took the compress she had used earlier. He added another piece of rag. He went to the door and unbarred it, bracing himself against the cold.

"What the devil?" came Tayback's voice, slurred with sleep.

Dawn was slowly illuminating the hills, Tom saw. The lowering gray skies gave little hope of sunshine, however. The wind had indeed died, although it was still strong enough to swirl fallen snow among the white-shrouded trees. Very little new snow seemed to be falling. Hastily he packed snow into the pieces of cloth and retreated to the cabin's warmth.

Sharon gave him a strained smile of thanks as she accepted the compresses. She laid one gently against Stever's forehead, then began to sponge his face with the other one. She appeared to sink into total absorption in her task.

Tom left her at it and saw to Tayback. The big outlaw was awkward and surly, clearly aching from his confinement. Tom felt a little sympathy, but he was careful to keep Tayback under the barrels of the Greener.

"This isn't enough," Sharon said helplessly when he went back to her. "He needs real medical attention."

Tom hunkered beside her. Stever muttered incoherently

and tried to lift his unwounded arm. Sharon pressed it firmly back down at his side.

"We've got to get help," she said insistently. "I think he'll die if we don't."

Tom knew she was right. "We can try to get him to Konowa," he suggested, "but it'll be a hard trail." In his heart he was sure they could never make it, not with a wounded man and Ned Tayback in tow.

"Konowa's too far," Sharon moaned. She appeared to share his pessimism. Then her face brightened. "The mission! We can take him to the mission."

"Sacred Heart?" Tom said blankly.

She nodded eagerly. "It's much closer than Konowa, isn't it?"

Tom nodded mutely, assessing her idea.

"Well, then it's settled," she announced firmly.

"Do they have a doctor there?"

"No, but they have a clinic, and one of the sisters is trained as a nurse."

Tom jerked his head toward Tayback. "We can't drag him along to a mission school for girls."

"Why not?" she demanded. "He's a prisoner. He can't do anything as long as he's shackled, and he hasn't acted dangerous."

"His gang might come looking for him."

Indecision sharpened her features. She shook her head angrily. "We can't just let the marshal die without trying to get help!"

Grudgingly Tom had to admit she was right. Sacred Heart was the closest source of aid. The prospect of making the journey to the mission in the aftermath of the blizzard was daunting. But the alternatives were even more so. He could try to reach the mission on his own and return with help, but it was out of the question to leave Sharon here with Tayback and the wounded marshal. Nor could she hope to make the journey by herself through the snow. He didn't trust Tayback far enough to let him go free, even if he had been so inclined. Neither could he leave the outlaw manacled here to most likely die when the stove went out. There was no way around it. All four of them would have to go.

Grimly, he calculated the hazards of the trip. Under normal conditions reaching Sacred Heart would not have meant much more than a pleasant country jaunt. But these weren't normal conditions. Along with ministering to Stever, they would have to keep watch on Tayback.

But maybe the burly outlaw could be put to use, Tom thought. Whatever his past crimes, he seemed docile enough now.

"We can do it," Sharon's voice broke into his reverie. "We'll need some way to transport the marshal, though."

"A travois," Tom said absently.

"Yes, of course!" she exclaimed. "I'll get as much clothing and cover as I can find to bundle him up."

"We'll need to be bundled up some ourselves," Tom reminded.

"I know." She was already looking appraisingly about the room and evaluating its contents.

"You're a dang fool if you think you're dragging me along on this tinhorn ride!" Tayback burst out suddenly.

Sharon had begun bustling about their gear. Tom went to stand over Tayback, the Greener clamped under one arm. "Oh, you're going along," he assured him. "And I won't be dragging you. You offered to help once, and now I'm taking you up on it. You're going to be giving us a hand with the marshal."

CHAPTER 3

"WHAT do you think I am?" Tayback protested. "Some kind of slave or nurse or something?"

"Just pick up your end of the stretcher," Tom ordered coldly. "Like I told you, if you help us out now, I'll put in a good word for you when the time comes."

Tayback looked skeptically down at Stever's unconscious form bundled snugly on the makeshift stretcher. In his heavy coat, the outlaw bulked large in the small cabin. "This ain't no decent work for a man," he griped. "Carting sick folk around is for women."

"He's sick because one of your men shot him. Now pick it up, and don't try anything. I can put a slug in you before you could blink."

Tayback eyed him carefully. Tom was in his mackinaw, but he had it bunched up at the side so the butt of his Colt could come easily to hand. "I almost believe you could, cowdog," Tayback allowed grudgingly.

"You'll only have one chance to find out."

With a scowl of resentment Tayback stooped and gripped the poles of the stretcher in his big fists. He straightened effortlessly with his share of the weight. Tom glanced at Sharon. Clad in her coat, she stood well to one side. Her lower lip was clenched between her teeth. She kept the Greener leveled in Tayback's direction.

Satisfied, Tom lifted his end of the crude stretcher. It consisted of an old blanket slung on ropes between two poles Tom had cut from saplings outside the cabin. It would also serve as a travois.

Only Stever's closed eyes showed above the kerchief they

had used to cover the lower part of his flushed, bearded face. Tom had tied him securely to the travois, and he looked like more of a prisoner than did Tayback. In order for the outlaw to be able to assist, Tom had been forced to release him from the handcuffs with the key he had taken from Stever's pocket. Tayback had shown little outright hostility, only a sour unwillingness to help prepare for their departure.

"Open the door and then stand clear," Tom directed Sharon.

She obeyed, and the cold washed into the cabin. "Move," Tom ordered.

Tayback shifted grips so he was facing forward, and together they carried the stretcher from the cabin. Tom had been out earlier to cut the poles and saddle the horses. But the cold was still a brutal shock to his body.

The storm had ended, although low-hanging clouds threatened more snow and made it a dark gloomy morning. Occasional gusts of wind swirled miniature blizzards from the drifted snow. The landscape rolled away in irregular slopes and mounds of white, concealing the true contours of the ground beneath. Tom's gaze roamed over the shapes of trees drooping under burdens of snow or swept clean by the erratic wind. They created strange weird forms against the pale barren background. His shiver was born of more than the cold. Travel in this eerie world would be hazardous.

The four saddled horses were tied close together at the edge of the woods. They shifted and snorted their displeasure as they saw the humans. Tom's earlier passage had already flattened a trail of sorts, but the footing was still uncertain. He found himself having to watch his step as well as keep a cautious eye on Tayback slogging stolidly ahead of him. On the stretcher Stever stirred and groaned as if the cold had penetrated even his fevered senses.

As they neared the horses, Tom glanced back to confirm Sharon's presence. She was close behind them, still carrying the Greener to cover the prisoner.

"Hold up, Tayback."

The outlaw halted and looked over his shoulder. "You mean we ain't going to *carry* him all the way to the mission?" he asked sarcastically.

"Put the stretcher down easy and move away from it."

Tom lowered his own end so they set the stretcher down together. Without looking back, Tayback trudged away through the snow.

"That's far enough!" Tom snapped. "Turn around!"

Tayback turned back. "Just going for a stroll," he said with his old grin.

"Keep an eye on him," Tom told Sharon.

He went back to the travois and secured it so it would drag behind Stever's sorrel gelding. The animal accepted the odd burden with only a few tosses of its head and a suspicious stare directed at Tom's activities.

The horses had already been loaded with everything salvagable from the cabin in the way of supplies and clothing. The findings had been meager.

Tom returned one last time to make sure the fire and the stove were out and to be certain they weren't leaving behind anything of use. He pulled the door shut carefully as he left. Maybe the cabin would again provide sanctuary for some future needy wayfarers. It had certainly saved their lives the night before. Of course, Tom told himself darkly, they might not survive the day ahead.

He put Tayback in the lead on his big roan and positioned himself next on Paint where he could keep an eye on the prisoner. Tayback's horse would be doing the hardest work of breaking the trail, but the roan looked sturdy enough. There would be plenty of time to worry about the animal playing out, when and if it happened. In the meantime, Tayback would be at a disadvantage on a winded horse if he tried to make a break.

Sharon was next in the procession. She had the duty of holding a close watch on their patient in his crude transport.

The reins of Stever's trailing horse were snubbed to her saddlehorn.

"Move out," Tom called ahead.

Obediently Tayback urged his horse forward. A cold gust of wind stirred Paint's mane as he followed the roan, stepping high in the hock-deep snow. Tom spared one glance rearward to check on Sharon's start. She was sitting her mare easily, her body swaying with the animal's movements. She had twisted about to see how the travois traveled. Turning forward, she caught Tom's glance. Her face was muffled beneath her scarf, but he thought she smiled. He turned his attention once more to Tayback.

"You just tell me which direction to go, cowdog, and I'll do her," the outlaw flung back over his shoulder.

Tom didn't waste breath answering.

"Can you find the mission?" Sharon had asked Tom earlier in the cabin.

"I think so," he had told her. "I know pretty much where it is from here."

He hadn't added that the heavy snowfall might well conceal any landmarks. He figured she already knew that, and if she didn't, then there was no point having her fret about it. They had to try for the mission. There was no other choice.

The rolling terrain made progress uncertain. The horses scrambled up snow-layered hills, half slid down steep slopes, and lunged their way through heavy drifts. Soon all of the animals were sweating despite the cold. Thin sheets of ice formed on them, then sloughed away beneath the bunching and swelling of their straining muscles.

"My nag can't keep breaking trail forever," Tayback warned as they crested a ridge beneath the skeletal limbs of a stand of scrub oak. "He'll go down and you'll lose him if you ain't careful. Then we'll be short a horse."

"You'll be short a horse," Tom corrected in a growl. "Keep moving. And don't fret. I won't work your horse to death. He's got plenty left in him yet."

Tayback muttered under his breath and kicked the roan forward with sudden violence. The animal plunged down the slope in front of them. Wind had scoured clean much of the rocky incline and allowed patches of ice to form. Squatting on its hunches, forelegs stiffened in front of it, the roan slid down the slope. Tayback sat his saddle with an expert's grace, surprising in a rider of his bulk.

"Be careful!" Tom yelled back at Sharon, then put his horse after Tayback.

Surefooted as a puma, Paint skittered sideways down the slope. Behind him, Tom heard Sharon's sudden cry of alarm. He jerked his head around in time to see the travois slew to the side of Stever's horse as the animal started down the slope in Sharon's wake. One of the bindings had come loose. The crude stretcher banged hard against a sturdy sapling then whiplashed back the other way. Stever's horse, panicked, gave a great lunge as if to escape the unstable burden it towed.

The sorrel's precipitous rush down the slope carried it past Sharon. Tom glimpsed the animal's wildly rolling eyes, the long streamer of saliva trailing from its mouth, and hauled up hard on his reins. Responding, Paint stiffened his legs, managing to slow but not stop their descent. Tom leaned far from his saddle as the sorrel drew level. He stretched himself into the effort as he clamped the barrel of Paint's body with his legs.

The gloved fingers of his reaching hand managed to close on the whipping reins as the sorrel plunged past him. He jerked his fist in a tight circle, looping the reins around his wrist, and hauled back hard. The tightening of the reins almost jerked him from his saddle. Paint was dancing frantically to maintain his balance. Tom had an instant's view of the stretcher almost beneath the feet of the horses as he and his mount were dragged down the slope by the sorrel's momentum.

With thrashing legs Stever's sorrel caught its balance as it skidded onto the level ground at the base of the slope. Paint gave an agile twist that carried him and his rider past the animal. The travois and its burden came to a cockeyed halt behind the sorrel. Tom was off Paint in an instant. He still held the reins of Stever's horse. It shied away from him, then calmed as he extended a gentling hand.

Sharon's mare reached the bottom of the slope with a clattering of hooves. She had taken the descent almost as fast as the panicked sorrel. Springing from her saddle, she dropped to her knees beside the travois as the sorrel steadied under Tom's hand.

Tom snapped a look about. Tayback had halted his horse and was gazing back at the accident. He seemed on the verge of kicking his big roan into flight down the draw that skirted the base of the slope.

"Hold it, Tayback!" Tom shouted fiercely. "You won't outrun a bullet!"

Tayback wheeled his horse back around. The expression on his face was open and innocent, but his eyes were hooded. Tom understood that he had deliberately taken the slope too fast in hopes of causing just the sort of accident as had taken place.

"Get off your horse!" he ordered furiously and pulled his Colt to back up the command.

Tayback dismounted. He eyed Tom carefully.

"Over there under that tree and sit down." Tom gestured with the Colt's long barrel.

"Yessir." Tayback made a great show of scrambling to obey.

Tom watched him with a scowl. Gun still in hand, he looked down at Sharon by Stever's side.

"He's still alive, praise God!" she exclaimed softly. "And I don't think his wound opened up, either."

The cold itself might've helped keep the wound closed, Tom guessed. And, other than that first impact with the tree, the sliding descent of the travois, though uncontrolled, should not have been particularly jarring. The slick steepness of the slope would've seen to that.

"You know we'll never make it hauling a wounded man along," Tayback spoke from his position beneath the tree. "He'll slow us up and we'll all freeze to death. No point in wasting three lives for one."

"Shut up," Tom said tightly.

"Just pointing out plain facts. You'd best listen."

"You'd best not try another stunt like that, or I'll see you never make it to the mission. You savvy?"

"What stunt?" Tayback objected. "My horse got away from me, is all."

Sharon had resettled Stever in the travois. She straightened the coat and blankets insulating him, then checked the ropes that held him in place. "I'm sorry," she apologized, looking up at Tom. "I had the reins snubbed. They came loose when the horse bolted." She drew the scarf from her face. Her piquant features were troubled.

"Forget it," Tom advised. "Nothing you could've done."

He offered her a hand and drew her up to her feet. For a moment they were very close. Her cheeks were flushed from the cold. Tom let go of her gloved hand and stepped past her to see to the travois. He retied the binding that had worked loose, this time making certain it was secure.

If the brush with disaster had been anyone's fault, he mused bitterly, it had been his. He had let things get out of his control. He could not afford to make such mistakes. Had Tayback's actions been deliberate, as he suspected? Had the outlaw really tried to engineer an accident? And was Tayback right about their chances for survival in this hostile wilderness? The ceaseless cold made even thinking hard. Icy fists seemed to grip his skull with ever increasing pressure.

He ordered Tayback once more into the saddle, then swung up himself. He watched Tayback closely as they set out again, but the outlaw eased his horse forward with almost mincing steps, as if determined to prove his lack of duplicity.

A gust of wind swept a cloud of snow over them. For a moment Tayback's bulky shape was all but obscured. Then he drifted back into view. Tom cocked an eye at the lowering clouds. The last of the blowing flakes of snow teared his vision, and he blinked his eyes clear. The clouds were lower than they had been earlier, he decided. He didn't like their looks.

The cold and the snow and the threatening clouds seemed to be all there was in the world. Single file, they threaded their way over and around the wooded hills as the day crawled on.

Glancing back, Tom could see Sharon as a small muffled figure sitting her mare against a ghostly backdrop of rugged white terrain and clawing skeletal trees. Cold had crept through his layers of clothing into every crevice of his body. Tayback's horse plodded ahead of him. Its rider appeared immune to the frigid conditions.

Abruptly the outlaw's roan humped his back wildly. Tayback's startled yell rang out. Rider and horse dropped from sight, having stepped off into an unseen drift that threatened to swallow them both.

The roan's plunging legs could clearly find no immediate purchase beneath the snow. Tayback, reeling with the frantic bucking of horse, clung desperately to the saddle. Then the roan lurched over sideways, half burying its rider in the enveloping snow. Tayback's arms flailed.

Tom urged Paint delicately forward. He could see where the roan's tracks dropped off into the drift, and drew Paint up several feet shy of that spot. He fumbled at the lariat on his saddle, his hands numb inside his gloves. The rope was stiff and inflexible in the cold.

A loop was already set in it. Tom had been a cowhand for too long to ever carry a rope that wasn't ready for use. He put it into a clumsy twirl above his head. Its stiffness, and the confining weight of his heavy clothing, made his efforts awkward. If he missed with his first throw, Tayback might well be swallowed up by the snow before he could throw again.

"Tayback!" he shouted, and made his cast.

The outlaw heard his yell. He looked up with frantic eyes and saw the loop descending upon him. It settled wide around him. He grabbed for it like a drowning man. Tom gave him time to get it under his arms, then he gently tugged it firm and snubbed a turn around his saddlehorn.

Paint was a cow pony. Even in hock-deep snow, with a man on the other end of the rope, he knew what to do. He backed until the rope was taut. At Tom's urging, he continued to shuffle backward over the trampled snow. Tom was aware of Sharon on her mare to one side of him, watching breathlessly.

Slowly Tayback was drawn away from his thrashing roan and clear of the drift. Panting, he scrambled to his feet, shrugging out of the rope. He brushed at the snow which clung to him.

"My horse!" he waved a hand back at the floundering animal. Whether it was real concern for the animal or worry about his own welfare, Tom didn't know, but the emotion seemed genuine enough.

Only the roan's head and pawing forelimbs were free of the snow now. Its efforts to escape had only bogged it deeper in the yielding drift. How deep could the snow be? Tom wondered. He had a sudden ugly mental image of the horse's frozen body buried in the drift until the spring thaw.

Automatically he had recoiled the rope. He set it to twirling again. Paint, sensing the movement, went rigid. It gave Tom a platform as solid as stone from which to make his cast.

The loop dropped to the churned snow, encircling the wild-eyed head of the panicked roan. Tom pulled it snug around the horse's neck. As if sensing that help was near, the roan lessened its struggles, although its eyes still rolled wildly. The animal's hindquarters were toward Tom.

"Tayback! Find the edge of the drift so I can work around

in front of your horse. If I try to pull him loose from here, I'll haul him over backward."

Tayback grunted his understanding. He pulled up a thick branch from where it protruded out of the snow. Using it as a probe, he carefully skirted the drift.

"Okay!" he shouted finally from a position near the roan's head.

Keeping the rope taut, Tom edged Paint around the drift until he was in front of the trapped animal. "Stay behind me and don't let me back off into another drift," he snapped over his shoulder.

Carefully he worked Paint rearward. The wiry mustang was smaller than the roan and probably could not have pulled the other animal free as a deadweight. But if the roan could be drawn close enough to the edge of the drift for its hooves to find purchase, then maybe it could scramble free with the assistance of Paint's strength.

The roan began to struggle against the tightening pull of the loop. Beneath him Tom could feel Paint's muscles bunching and trembling with the strain. The mustang was almost squatting as Tom worked him backward.

Slowly, despite its struggles, the roan was inched forward through the snow. Tom knew the moment its forefeet found purchase. He could feel it through the tension on the rope and the increased speed of Paint's steps. At last the roan stopped fighting the noose. It hurled itself forward against the imprisoning snow.

A flailing hoof broke clear. The roan's shoulders heaved up into view. Then the rope sagged briefly slack before Paint could tauten it. Tom eased the mustang off as the roan clambered the rest of the way up onto solid footing.

Tom felt Paint sag beneath him. Instantly he slid out of the saddle. Tayback was lumbering toward the roan, lifting his booted feet high to clear the snow. The roan stood on trembling legs, its head lowered. Breaths of steam puffed from its nostrils. It made no effort to shake the coat of snow from its body.

Tom slogged closer as Tayback examined the animal. The outlaw straightened and shuffled around to face him. "He's winded bad," he managed through chattering teeth. "He's got to rest!"

Tom knew he was right. And Tayback himself needed a respite. The heat of his body would rapidly melt some of the snow still clinging to his clothing. In the frigid air the moisture would refreeze. If his clothes weren't given a chance to dry out, Tayback would literally catch his death of cold.

Tom cast about. A great pile of boulders, some as large as a house, made a giant bulky mound a hundred yards distant. He glanced at Paint. The mustang was in little better shape than the roan. He had put the animal to cruel effort.

"Let's try for those boulders," he directed. "Maybe there's some shelter on yonder side of them."

He and Tayback led their mounts. He refused to let Sharon give up her mare to either of them, despite her insistent offers. Tayback was beginning to shiver uncontrollably by the time they rounded the pile of boulders.

Tom mouthed a silent prayer of thanks at what he saw. The vagaries of the wind had swept clear a secluded niche beneath two boulders propped against one another. The naked limbs of a dead fallen tree jutted up from the snow nearby. They had found their sanctuary.

Once they got a fire started with the dead branches, the trapped body heat of themselves and their animals in the close confines of the niche made it almost cozy. Stever's condition seemed unchanged. Tom guessed the marshal had lapsed into the stupor that could precede death by days or mere hours.

Tayback's shaking gradually ceased as he huddled near the fire. Tom handcuffed him just to be safe. "You saved my life, cowdog," he offered from across the flames.

"I did the same for your horse," Tom reminded.

"Well, then I guess we both owe you a debt." Tayback snorted laughter.

Something rang hollow in his stubborn affability. Beside Tom, Sharon shivered. "You helped out some," Tom growled at Tayback. "Just call us even."

Sharon laid her hand suddenly on Tom's arm. "Oh, no." She was gazing out of the niche. White specks danced in the air: the snow had started to fall again.

"We need to move out." Tom forced himself to shift away from the warmth of the fire. "We can't afford to let any more snow pile up."

He ducked out of the niche and stared up from beneath his Stetson at the grim sky. Sometime past noon, he figured. How many miles had they come? While crossing the snowy terrain, it had been hard to estimate distance. But he reckoned they still had a mite further to go.

He saw Sharon look regretfully back at the niche when they rode out. The cold seemed more bitter than ever with the memory of the fire flickering in his mind. The new snow didn't let up. It continued to fall lightly until a whitish haze seemed to lay across Tom's vision.

He tried not to think of Stever being pulled behind on the travois. The marshal would have had no chance at all back at the cabin, he told himself, and there was no going back. Either the marshal made it or he didn't. The same, he thought darkly, could be said for them all.

More than once he ordered a halt while Tayback, his hands now free, dismounted and probed the snow in front of them with a long branch, testing for other treacherous drifts. After his first few complaints, the outlaw performed the duty without protest.

As he sat his horse watching Tayback probe yet another seemingly innocent expanse of snow beyond a small grove of saplings, Tom tried to picture the sun hidden above the dense clouds. He felt as though they had been trudging and floundering across this frigid wasteland for an eternity. Once again he gazed at the sky. The afternoon was well along now, and the winter darkness would come soon. Had his calculations been wrong? Had they unknowingly passed by the mission in the snow? Were they any closer to it now than they had been when they left the warmth and security of the cabin? They would never survive a night without shelter.

Tayback gave a muffled cry that snapped Tom's attention back to reality. Probing with the thick limb, Tayback had gone up to his thigh in the snow.

"Give me a hand here!" he shouted.

Tom started Paint forward. The naked trunks of the saplings between him and Tayback made casting his rope impossible.

"Keep the horse back, dang it!" Tayback howled. "This is all liable to go down with us!" He struggled without success to pull his leg free. "You'll have to come over here!"

Gingerly Tom dismounted. He recalled the earlier drift that had almost consumed man and animal alike. He snubbed the roan's reins to his saddlehorn. Treading in Tayback's footprints, he went forward, easing between the saplings. He extended an assisting hand to Tayback as he came into reach.

Something in Tayback's eyes warned him, but it was too late. The outlaw came surging erect, sweeping the branch around in a full arc. Tom tried to duck his head behind his hunching shoulder. His fingers clawed reflexively at his Colt. He was too slow. The limb, brittle with cold, splintered against his shoulder and jolted him sideways. His half-drawn Colt dropped from sight in the snow. Tayback gave a bestial howl and flung the remaining fragment of the branch aside. He lunged at Tom, trying to choke him.

Tom fell back under the weight of the assault. Sharon's scream rang in his ears. He glimpsed Tayback's face. Gone was the easygoing temperament. In its place was a brute fury. Tom realized that Tayback's earlier demeanor was all a sham, a facade meant to conceal a dark predatory nature.

His gullibility could cost him and Sharon and the marshal their lives.

Tom's head was jammed backwards down into the snow, his Stetson lost. The snow clogged his mouth and nose with icy pressure. Tayback's hands were tight on his throat. Tom heard Sharon's muffled voice as she cried out again. He knew Tayback was too close to him for Sharon to risk using the shotgun. It was up to him.

Desperately he bucked against Tayback's crushing weight. His gloved hands groped for and caught the outlaw's thick wrists. Half-buried in the snow, he jerked his knees up so they collided with Tayback's solid rump. At the same time he wrenched hard against Tayback's wrists. The bulk of the outlaw was catapulted off him and to one side.

Tom came lurching up from the snow. Instinctively, he struck out blindly, and his knuckles caught Tayback's ear. The outlaw's flailing fist landed hard on Tom's face. He reeled, but the knee-deep snow kept him on his feet. Through blurred vision, he saw Tayback's looming form. Without thinking, he ducked and heard the swish of Tayback's swing pass overhead.

Tom delivered a volley of blows, but Tayback, whose body was protected by a coat and layers of clothing, only grunted at the blows.

Only a fool or a desperate man used his head as a weapon—Tom felt like both. He lunged forward and butted Tayback in the midriff. Straightening, he lifted an uppercut at the jaw. It missed as Tayback reared back from the head butt. Now the snow helped keep him on his feet, as it had Tom. He lurched to regain his balance, and Tom swung again. He felt awkward and clumsy, hampered by his layers of clothing and the difficulty of maintaining his footing. His fist bounced harmlessly off Tayback's padded shoulder.

The outlaw roared like some beast and lunged again with grappling arms. There could be no fancy evasive footwork in the snow. Tom tried to dodge, and stumbled. He landed a glancing blow on Tayback's jaw before the powerful arms clamped about him.

Even through his clothing he felt the brutal power of Tayback's practiced grip. This was no simple bearhug, but a cruel wrestling hold that imprisoned one arm and bent him painfully backward. Unbroken, the hold would cripple him for certain.

He felt his spine twisted agonizingly. Tayback's panting snarls sounded in his ear. The outlaw had his face buried in Tom's chest, where Tom's groping fingers could not reach his eyes.

Frantically Tom tore at the kerchief binding Tayback's Stetson to his head. He ripped the material away and clapped the palm of his free hand full against Tayback's exposed ear. He could tell by the shudder of the big man's body that he had been hurt. Again he slapped his palm against the ear, and again. Tayback jerked his head back to escape the percussive impacts.

A fool or a desperate man. . . . Tom smashed his forehead down between Tayback's glaring eyes. The impact jolted his own brain, but he felt that powerful grip loosen. Tom wrenched his imprisoned arm free. Lifting both hands overhead, he pounded the edges of his clenched fists squarely down on the bridge of Tayback's nose.

The double blow would've staggered a horse. Tayback let him go, and retreated a pace, shaking his head. Tom stepped after him. The snow beneath them had finally been pounded flat by their trampling feet. It gave Tom a surface for some footwork. And he had Tayback's range.

He snapped the outlaw's head sideward with his right, jolted it back with his left. Tayback lashed at him with both fists. Tom leaned his torso clear, then shifted back in and rammed his fist against Tayback's sore ear. He didn't waste time on Tayback's body beneath its protective layers of clothing. Instead, he went for the jaw and the skull.

Tayback rocked backward beneath the blows. He lifted his

thick arms in front of his face for protection. Tom had an instant in which to set himself. On braced legs he rammed an uppercut beneath the blocking arms, putting the whole lift of his body behind it. His fist caught Tayback's jaw and drove his head back so that his face was tilted to the sky. Tom caught his balance to keep from toppling over with the follow-through of the blow.

Tayback pivoted in a drunken half-circle and fell on his face in the snow. Tom pounced on him like a puma on a wounded bull. He jammed Tayback's face down into the snow. He felt Tayback's powerful body surge up beneath him. He gritted his teeth and locked his arms rigid, forcing Tayback's face deeper. For a moment he felt like he was on a bucking bronc. Then Tayback's struggles began to weaken. Grimly Tom rode the big man. Only when his struggles ceased did he ease himself clear.

With an effort he heaved Tayback over so the outlaw could breathe. Spread-eagled in the snow, Tayback didn't move.

He reeled to his feet, only to feel his knees start to buckle immediately. Then Sharon's strong hands caught him and drew him up with surprising strength.

CHAPTER 4

SISTER Mary Agnes lifted her head and sighed. Her fingers were beginning to ache from writing laboriously with the quill pen. Carefully she set the instrument aside. Who would've believed that twenty-five Indian girls, three nuns, and an elderly caretaker at a remote mission school could generate so much paperwork? But there always seemed to be reports to be filed with the Church or the government, as well as requisitions for supplies and evaluations of the scholastic and spiritual status of her charges.

And, of course, she was forced to admit, she had been remiss in letting the paperwork pile up. In that sense, the blizzard had seemed like a heaven-sent opportunity for her to make amends and catch up on the backlog.

But after hours spent squinting at her own precise lettering in the poor illumination of the oil lamps and the window of her study, she was ready for an end to the snowfall and a return to the normal routine of the school.

But that was not to be, she realized ruefully as she peered out of the window. Sometime during the afternoon, while she had bent over her work in stubborn concentration, it had begun to snow again. Not heavily, but any snow at all was too much on top of the two-foot accumulation that had already effectively isolated the mission.

Watching the flakes drifting past the window now made her shiver. It was cold inside the massive stone building. The coal-fed furnaces in the cellar three stories below and the foot warmers in the rooms were inadequate to heat the big building in cold such as they had been experiencing over the past two days.

For the time being, the Sacred Heart Mission was a microcosm cut off from the rest of the world. She may as well continue with the paperwork, she reflected. Sister Lenora and Sister Ruth should be able to see to the girls once classes were ended. The strict regimen of duties and activities that she herself had established for the students reduced decisions by other staff members to a minimum.

And there would be another staff member soon, she mused. No doubt the new teacher—Sharon Easton—was stranded in Konowa, awaiting transport to the mission. Well, she would just have to wait until Isaac could get a wagon out to fetch her. Mary Agnes hoped the young woman would be suitable for her role here. She was not altogether sure she approved of this new policy of hiring laypersons as teachers for the school.

However, Miss Easton's qualifications were quite satisfactory, and her correspondence had the right blend of zeal and submissiveness. Perhaps Miss Easton would serve well enough during however long she stayed. Mary Agnes predicted with fatalistic certainty that the young woman would inevitably give up her teaching career to marry some local farmer or cowhand and live the demanding life of a frontier bride.

But whatever happened, she reminded herself, the Lord would continue to provide, just as He had done since she had taken on the responsibility for this remote school and its female students five years before.

The students, she mused. Her girls. Her flock. They came and went, the presence of any one of them dictated by the government, the tribal leaders, and the student herself. Some came because life at the mission was better than life on the reservations. Others viewed the school as little more than a white man's prison into which they had been cast. And then there were the few who honestly hungered to learn.

She had found satisfaction in working with this latter group, in seeing them grow and mature into fine Christian women. Frequently, after completing their studies, they would remain for a time to work at the school. Their simple presence did more to draw their sisters off the reservations and to the mission than the combined efforts of herself, her assistants, and the U.S. government.

Yes, there was a satisfaction to her work here, she reflected, a satisfaction that made all the hardship and heartbreak, and even the occasional danger, more than worthwhile.

"Sister Mary Agnes." The summons pulled her mind abruptly back to her cold gloomy study. "Come quickly. There are strangers outside!"

Sister Ruth's oval face bore her customary look of perplexed concern with which she met most new situations. Although older than Mary Agnes, she always seemed grateful to look to the younger woman for guidance at such times.

"Strangers?" Mary Agnes heard her own surprised voice as she rose automatically. "In this weather?"

Sister Ruth nodded emphatically. "Four horses and what looks like a stretcher being pulled behind one of them!"

"Very well. Let's go." She shared some of Ruth's perplexity. Together they hurried down the dark corridor and descended the steep stone stairway. "Where is Sister Lenora?" Mary Agnes asked over her shoulder as they reached the second-floor landing.

"With the girls in the dormitory." Ruth anticipated Sister Mary Agnes's next question and said, "All are accounted for."

"Good." Mary Agnes nodded her satisfaction. The safety of her flock was her first consideration. In this remote area, brigands and outlaws were not unknown, although few had ever offered any threat to the school. But, whatever the identity of these strangers, if they had been long out in this cold, they would be in desperate need of succor.

She was moving at a brisk pace, her habit swinging about her legs, as she reached the ground floor. Sister Ruth hurried to keep up. Slightly breathless, Mary Agnes halted before the massive oak doors and pulled open the tiny viewing portal to peer out. Cold air struck her face like a slap. She squinted automatically. Through the light snow she could see the four horses as Ruth had described them. The party had passed the farthest outbuildings. They were making their arduous way toward the front doors. Aside from the exhaustion evident in the sagging forms of horses and riders alike, she could make out few details.

Decisively she shut the viewing portal and reached for a cloak on the nearby stand. She swept it about her shoulders and adjusted the hood over her head. Then she braced herself and pulled the near door open. The cold seemed to explode into the dark hallway. She lowered her head and plunged out into it. The cape would offer scant protection if she had to stay outside for very long.

The four horses were very near now. She was thankful that Isaac had shoveled paths between the main structure and the scattered outbuildings. He would be nearby, she knew, keeping watch on the newcomers. That knowledge gave her reassurance.

The riders approached single file through one of the cleared paths. As they drew near, Mary Agnes felt her eyes widen. The leader was a lanky cowboy sagging atop a drooping spotted horse. Behind him, an ungainly figure was draped like a sack of potatoes across a big roan dusted white with snow. The third rider was distinguishable only as a small, heavily bundled figure. A fourth horse pulled some burden.

The leader pawed clumsily with a gloved hand at the bandanna covering his face. He pulled it down to reveal lean features, blue and gaunt with cold. His mouth worked, and Mary Agnes realized his face was too numb for him to speak. Despite herself, she took an impulsive step forward.

At last the rider found words. "We've got a wounded U.S. marshal and his prisoner, and a young woman near froze to death," he managed. "Before God, Sister, we need your help."

"Tom? Are you awake?" a soft voice called out insistently through the heavy door.

Tom fumbled groggily up out of sleep. He had no immediate memory of how he had come to be in the narrow bed in this Spartan room. Pale, cold morning light issued through a single window.

"Tom? Are you up yet?"

He recognized Sharon's voice and sat up. He was in his long johns, he realized. He couldn't go to the door like that. The stone floor was cold on his naked feet even through the thin throw rug. He looked about for his clothes, but spotted only his hat atop a heavy wardrobe that filled one corner of the room. He clamped the Stetson on his head—it was better than nothing.

Cautiously he cracked the door and peered around its edge, careful to let only his head be visible.

Sharon's scrubbed face and china blue eyes gazed at him expectantly. "Oh!" she exclaimed softly. "Good morning."

"Morning," Tom mumbled.

Sharon dropped her eyes to the floor. A blush was spreading up her features. She wore a simple unadorned dress of neutral color that had the look of a uniform. She stumbled before getting words out. "Sister Mary Agnes would like to see you—us."

"She the boss?"

Sharon gave a quick nod and kept her eyes downcast.

"Oh. Well, I, uh, better get dressed," Tom stammered.

"Okay. I'll be down the hall!" Sharon said in a rush. She turned quickly away in apparent relief.

Tom shut the door and shook his head. It didn't help. He still felt groggy. He realized there were several questions he could've asked Sharon, but he hadn't thought of them in time and she would probably have been too embarrassed to answer them, anyway.

"Sister Mary Agnes," he said aloud in a wondering tone.

There was a washbasin, and he felt some refreshed after using it briefly. He found his clothes folded neatly in the wardrobe. They had obviously been cleaned while he slept. He guessed a full night had passed.

His gunbelt was coiled on another shelf in the wardrobe. He hesitated, then thought of Tayback and strapped it on. A gun might not be proper dress in a girls school, but he felt better having it at his hip.

He pulled the Colt and checked it. Surprisingly it looked to have been cleaned. He hadn't had a chance to do much beyond try to dry it off after recovering it from the snow following his fight with Tayback.

Memory of the struggle brought to life various aches in his body. His recollection of the period after the fight was vague. With Sharon's help, he had managed to bind Tayback's unconscious bulk across the roan before they had set out again. Dim images of riding numbly through the snow shifted in his mind. After ages, he had seen the great gabled edifice rising darkly out of the snowy terrain ahead. Its significance has been beyond him until Sharon cried out that they had reached the mission.

He did remember speaking briefly from horseback to a tall imposing woman in nun's dress who had emerged from the massive front doors of the mission. That must have been Sister Mary Agnes.

Fully dressed, he paused to peer out the window of his room. A bleak snowy landscape greeted his gaze. The shrouded white shapes of a few outbuildings were visible. He figured his window was at least three stories above the ground.

Sharon hurried up to him as he stepped into the dark hallway. Windows at either end provided illumination. There were niches for oil lamps to be used at night.

"Come on," Sharon urged. She reached as if to catch his hand, then snatched her own fingers back.

Tom frowned at her. "This Sister Mary Agnes is a bearcat, is she?" he drawled.

"Oh!" Sharon grasped in surprise. "Why, no. She's nice, I suppose. I spoke with her a few moments when we arrived. She just makes me a little nervous, I guess. After all, I will be working for her, and I need to make a good impression."

"Relax. You'll do fine," Tom told her, grinning.

Her smile flashed briefly. "I'm glad you'll be with me."

"What about the marshal and Tayback?"

"Marshal Stever is resting. One of the nuns is looking after him. She's a nurse, like I told you."

"And Tayback?" The idea of the outlaw here at the girls school was an ugly one. Tom remembered the swift change from tail-wagging hound dog to savage wolf.

"He's locked up somewhere. Someone named Isaac is supposed to be watching him."

Tom felt a sudden urgency to see to things. With Stever stove up by his wound, he supposed he himself was in charge of the prisoner. "Let's go meet the Sister."

"I talked to one of the other nuns some this morning," Sharon explained as she led the way. "Sister Ruth. She's sweet. She came and told me Sister Mary Agnes wanted to see us both when we were up. She says the mission is snowed in completely, and they don't expect to hear from anyone until the snow melts."

Tom lengthened his stride. Sharon moved faster to keep from being outdistanced. She led him down two steep flights of stone stairs. Tom saw no sign of any of the school's students. At his query, Sharon told him they were already in their morning classes.

On the ground floor they passed a large unoccupied dining hall and a parlor. The classrooms were on this floor also, Sharon told him.

She halted in front of an ornate door. Lifting her fist, she hesitated, then knocked politely. Tom glanced at the nervous expression on her face. He felt some of his confidence slipping away. Disquietingly, he remembered facing an unforgiving school master for some boyish infraction of the rules during his youth.

"Come in," a woman's voice called.

This was evidently the office of Sister Mary Agnes, Tom decided as they entered. Automatically he doffed his hat. The woman he remembered vaguely from their arrival the evening before was just rising from behind an oak desk. Two straight-backed chairs faced it. A crucifix was the only wall adornment.

"Good morning." Her smile softened the reserved contours of her face, but it vanished almost as quickly as it had come. "I'm Sister Mary Agnes, the headmistress here. Miss Easton has told me that your name is Tom Langston."

"Yes, ma'am."

"Please sit down."

She resumed her own seat as he obeyed. Sharon hesitated, then followed suit. For a moment Tom felt the sister's perceptive gaze taking his measure. He pushed aside his discomfort and opened his mouth to speak.

Before he could utter a word Sister Mary Agnes said, "I understand you are responsible for Miss Easton's safe arrival here, as well as Marshal Stever's survival and the continued captivity of the man Tayback. Miss Easton gives you a great deal of credit. Now that I've met you, I believe I can understand it a little better."

Tom shifted his weight awkwardly in the hard chair. He glanced at Sharon. She would not meet his gaze. He cleared his throat. "Things just kind of happened," he offered lamely. "I didn't do nothing special." He felt suddenly warm in the close confines of the office.

"But I think you did," Sister Mary Agnes stated. "Defeating that brute in hand-to-hand combat, leading a ragtag group to safety through these hills. Those things are very special, indeed."

"We were just lucky," Tom tried to protest.

"Nonsense. There is no true luck. The Lord brought you here. It was His will, or you would not have survived."

"Yes, ma'am."

"To my discredit, however, now that you are here, I am unable to determine what course to take." She paused thoughtfully after this admission.

Tom tried to make his mind work. Reaching the mission had become such an obsessive goal that he had literally not thought beyond achieving it.

"The safety of my flock here is, of course, my primary concern," the sister went on. "The presence of this outlaw is disturbing. You are certain he is Ned Tayback?"

"I'm certain," Tom answered. "He needs to be watched real close, ma'am—"

"He is in quite capable hands for the moment, I assure you," she cut him off. Abruptly she changed the subject. "Are you a man of faith, Mr. Langston?"

"I reckon I know Who's in charge, and I reckon I know my place in things."

"A good enough answer, I suppose. Mr. Langston, Sister Lenora tells me the marshal cannot travel in his condition, even if the weather conditions permitted. And I cannot justify simply releasing this man Tayback. To turn him out in the elements would be inhumane. Nor would I be able to take upon myself the responsibility of his further depredations should he somehow manage to continue his lawless ways once he was released."

Tom stirred. Her line of reasoning was similar to his own back at the cabin. "We didn't mean to bring no harm or danger to you or your school, ma'am," he apologized. "I hadn't thought very much on what we'd do once we got here. But now I figure maybe the best thing is for me to take

Tayback with me and head for Konowa. I can send some help back for the marshal."

"Tom, no! You can't!" Sharon said impulsively. She laid a hand on his arm, then drew it swiftly back with a quick glance at her headmistress.

Tom couldn't read a thing in the face of the older woman.

"I rather think Miss Easton is correct," she said however. "You are in no sort of condition to undertake such an expedition today, and probably not for several days in this kind of weather, particularly with the responsibility of keeping Mr. Tayback in custody. I understand he almost killed you on the trip here."

"I was trying to watch out for the marshal and Sharon, uh, Miss Easton," Tom explained. "It'd be different with just me and Tayback." He tried to force some assurance into his voice. From the look the Sister gave him, he figured he hadn't succeeded.

"I really do not think it would be wise for anyone to leave the mission until there is some improvement in the weather," she stated firmly. "We shall be safe enough here with Mr. Tayback in confinement, and yourself and Isaac to watch over him. I trust you will assist in that regard, Mr. Langston."

"Well, of course," Tom stammered. "But who is—?"

"Very well. It is settled," she cut off his words. "You shall remain here until it is safe for you to travel. At that time, you or Isaac will go to Konowa to secure medical aid for the marshal, as well as assistance to transport Mr. Tayback to a place of incarceration."

Tom drew a deep breath and exhaled slowly. "Tayback claims his gang will be looking for him, ma'am. Might be he's just blowing, but if he ain't, then it could be they'd manage to find their way here."

Sister Mary Agnes appeared to consider this for a time. "The word of a captive outlaw cannot be given a great deal of credit," she said at last. "And even if what he says is true, we can hardly let it affect our actions and decisions. The same considerations are present, regardless of whether his gang is a real or imaginary threat."

Tom shook his head in wordless admiration. There was iron in the woman. "Just the same, maybe we should post a lookout," he suggested.

"Of course. That would be a wise precaution. I shall leave the details to you and Isaac. I suppose some of the older girls would be able to assume the responsibility of keeping a watch, if necessary. I shall expect you and Isaac to keep me informed of your arrangements. Now, Mr. Langston, I really do need to visit with Miss Easton concerning her position and duties here. If you will please excuse us?"

"Yes, ma'am." Tom was getting used to saying that. "I'd like to check on Tayback and look in on Marshal Stever."

"Certainly. You'll find the infirmary at the far end of the second floor. We have incarcerated Mr. Tayback in a storeroom of the cellar."

"Thanks." Tom stood up clumsily. He cleared his throat. "Sister?"

"Yes, Mr. Langston?"

"We'd never have made it if it hadn't been for Miss Easton here. She's the one took care of the marshal and gave me a hand when I was most near dead from fighting with Tayback. I just thought you needed to know that."

"Thank you, Mr. Langston. Your insights are appreciated."

Once again Tom couldn't read what was behind the words. As he turned away, he caught Sharon's fleeting smile of gratitude.

In the corridor he clamped his Stetson back on his head. His stomach rumbled at him, and there was an unfamiliar wobble to his legs. He recalled the Sister's judgment that he was in no condition to undertake a journey across the snow-cloaked hills. Most likely she was right.

But his hunger and his weakness could wait. He plodded back up the stairs and wandered down the hallway. At its far end he spotted a door with a neat white cross painted on it.

As he drew near, it opened and a slender figure in a nun's habit bustled out, almost into his arms. She pulled up sharply with a startled gasp to avoid a collision. Tom had an impression of a young open face that was pretty, even framed in the austere attire of a nun.

"Oh, I'm sorry!" she exclaimed contritely. "I didn't see you!"

"I was looking for Marshal Stever," Tom said gruffly.

"He's in there." She gestured back at the door. "You're Mr. Langston, aren't you?" she rushed on then. "I'm Sister Lenora. I helped when you came in with Sharon and the marshal. I've been taking care of him. I was checking on him just now." Her enthusiasm fairly bubbled in her fast flow of words and her bright eyes.

"Pleased to meet you." Tom touched his hat brim. For some reason it didn't seem proper to return her unassuming smile. "How's the marshal doing?"

She pressed her lips together into a line. "He's asleep. I think the fever has broken, but he needs a lot of time to rest. I was up with him most of the night. I left one of the older girls in charge of my class while I came to check on him."

Tom could see the lines of exhaustion in her face now that she spoke of it. In her own way, he decided, this bright young nun had some iron in her also. "You're the nurse?"

"That's right. I run the infirmary when any of the girls get sick or have problems. But I've never treated a bullet wound like this before. I cleaned it, and then tried to manage the fever. He seems like a very strong man. Thank God the fever finally broke."

"Can I see him?"

"Oh, surely." She gave a flustered smile and made to get out of his path. "Just don't wake him up," she cautioned.

"I promise." Tom could no longer resist a smile at her earnest sincerity.

"You should get some rest, yourself," she advised seriously. "You really oughtn't to be out of bed yet."

"I'm all right. I'll get some rest after I check on the marshal."

She appeared satisfied. "Well, it was nice to meet you." She smiled quickly. "Now I've got to get back to my class." She scurried past him. "I'll check back on the marshal later this morning," she called over her shoulder.

Tom eased through the door into a sparsely furnished examination room. Through another door he saw Stever's supine figure in a bed. He went to the doorway and stood for a moment, studying the lawman.

Stever's bearded face was drawn and gaunt, but it no longer carried the deep flush of fever. The rise and fall of his chest beneath the blankets was steady and even.

Tom exhaled in relief. For the first time he let himself believe that the desperate gamble of transporting the wounded marshal across the icy wastes to the mission might've paid off. Stever was still badly injured, but Sister Lenora's professional care had succeeded in pulling him through the worst of it.

Quietly Tom withdrew. There was no sign of Sister Lenora in the corridor as he went back to the stairway. Descending past the ground floor, he found a heavy door leading into the cellar. A lantern and matches were set on a small shelf. He lit it and opened the door.

The lantern's glow illuminated a large storage chamber cluttered with discarded furniture and other debris. The air was cold and dank. The lantern light glistened off ice that had formed from the moisture seeping in from the outside walls.

The furnace room was off to his right; he could hear the confined roar of flames even through the panels of the door. Little, if any, of the heat reached this chamber.

Across the length of the cellar another lantern glowed. Tom touched the butt of his Colt instinctively. He threaded his way through the clutter toward the light. Before he reached it a figure rose up out of the gloom in his path.

Tom paused, lifting his own lantern higher. He kept his right hand near the Colt. He stared as a stooped figure in overalls and faded work shirt shuffled into view. The lantern's glow glinted off a seamed black face beneath curly salt-and-pepper hair. A heavy revolver was holstered on a ragged belt.

"Howdy, howdy," the old black man greeted in a rasping voice. "I figured you'd be down once the Sister got finished with you, so I just sat here and waited."

"You're Isaac," Tom said, lowering the lantern some.

"That's a fact. Isaac Jacob at your service." White teeth flashed in the dark face. He offered a calloused hand.

Taking it, Tom found his own hand gripped by fingers that were hard and gnarled like weathered wood. They possessed a surprising strength. "Tom Langston," he responded.

"Yessir, I know who you are. I done helped the sisters put you to bed. I expect you're feeling a mite better now?"

"Yeah. Thanks. The headmistress said you've got Tayback locked up down here?" Tom was trying to square the image of this old black man with the individual in whom Sister Mary Agnes placed such utter confidence.

"He's right back in there." A movement of his grizzled head indicated a door behind him. "Key's hanging there on the wall. I'll just let you go ahead and visit with him till your heart's content." Isaac chuckled. "I done used the marshal's handcuffs on him. I got him trussed up good to where he can't do much more'n complain. Granted, he's done a right amount of that."

"I'll bet."

"You just take your time." He paused and cocked his head. His sharp eyes appraised Tom shrewdly. "You done whipped that big ox?"

"Felt more like he whipped me," Tom confessed.

Isaac snorted with mirth and made his way on past. "You watch him, son," he advised. "He's a two-faced critter."

Whatever else he was, Isaac was a sharp judge of character,

Tom thought. He fitted the key in the lock, palmed his Colt, and pushed the door open.

It took him a moment to see Ned Tayback seated on the floor, his back to a corner of the bare room. The outlaw's right wrist had been shackled to his left ankle with the handcuffs, and his boots had been removed. Tom shook his head in grudging respect. Isaac hadn't been boasting. Secured in such a fashion, Tayback was virtually helpless.

"Is that you, cowdog?" Tayback blinked against the light. "I'm plumb thankful you're here. Look how that old coot chained me up, like I was some kind of animal!" He rattled the handcuffs. "Get these loose. This ain't no way to treat a civilized man."

"You ain't civilized," Tom drawled. "And I think that old man did a right pretty job of trussing you up."

Tayback turned and spat on the floor with an ugly sound. "I might've known I couldn't expect nothing better from no low-account cowdog who'd tie a man over his saddle and haul him through a blizzard. I almost froze my tail off, boy!"

"Would've saved us some trouble if you had."

Tayback glared balefully at him. "It'd save a whole lot more trouble if you'd just turn me loose right now."

Tom shook his head. "You're staying right here until I get some help from the law in Konowa to take you in proper."

"It won't happen. You won't live to see me brought in."

"Could be you're the one won't live to see it."

A look of furtive cunning came to Tayback's eyes. "That old coot tells me the marshal's still alive."

"Yeah, and getting better."

"But he still ain't up and around, is he? If he was, he'd have been down here to see me 'stead of you."

"He's mending fine."

"But he wouldn't be no good in a fight, would he? He won't be no help at all when my boys come to get me out of here."

"Your boys are probably happy to be rid of you," Tom asserted.

Tayback shook his head. "Don't you believe it! They'll come looking. My Segundo won't let me down. Besides, they're all too scared of what I'd do to them if they didn't come fetch me. What are you and the nuns and that old coot going to do when they show up? Serve them tea?"

"Maybe put a bullet in you and turn your carcass over to them," Tom said coldly.

"Not you, cowdog. You ain't going to shoot me down in cold blood. You're too soft."

"Soft enough to whip you."

"That's been bothering me a lot," Tayback confessed. "You don't look like nothing but skin and bones. I wouldn't have bet nothing that you could whip me in a rough and tumble."

"I didn't have any choice." Tom turned away. He had had enough of this brutal two-faced man.

"Hey, cowdog, don't you walk off from me like that!" Tayback snarled at his back. The outlaw's curses followed him as he left the cellar.

CHAPTER 5

ISAAC Jacob straightened from where he had been leaning against the wall as Tom mounted the stairs from the cellar. Isaac wore a battered old cavalry hat that sat on his head as if it were a part of him.

"I expect you've already looked in on the marshal," he greeted Tom.

Tom nodded. "Yeah." He gestured back down in the direction of Tayback's cell. "You did a good job with him."

Isaac shook his head. "You the one that brought him in. I'm just glad it wasn't me out there scrapping with him in the snow." He considered Tom a moment. "You hungry, son?"

"I could eat," Tom admitted.

"Well, come on. There's usually some leftovers down to the kitchen."

He led the way in his lumbering gait. It occurred to Tom that the old man was much stronger than he appeared.

In the kitchen Isaac rustled up some cold biscuits and bacon. Tom wolfed the food down hungrily and drank three mugs of cold fresh milk.

"You got your own milk cows here?" he questioned as he drained the last of the milk.

Isaac had been watching him appreciatively. "Cows and chickens. The cold's got the hens off their laying. They ain't used to it. But the cows are doing just fine. We also got a fair team of mules."

"You're the caretaker?" Tom leaned back contentedly in his chair.

"Aw, I help out some, and the Sister puts up with me, is all. I got me a little cabin out by the stable."

"Tayback says his men will come looking for him," Tom said, studying Isaac carefully. "There could be trouble."

Something stirred eagerly in the ancient eyes, but Isaac's tone was relaxed. "Is that a fact?"

Tom shrugged in answer.

Isaac's eyes dropped to Tom's holstered Colt. "Can you use that? You act like you wouldn't be comfortable walking around without it, but you ain't no hired gun."

"My pa taught me how to pull it without shooting my foot off, leastways."

"Your pa teach you how to whip Tayback, too?"

"He taught me some of what he knew."

"He must've been a good teacher."

"Who taught you?" Tom asked.

Humor sparkled in Isaac's eyes. "What do you mean by that, son?"

"I mean, who taught you how to fight? You and that cannon you're packing look to be old friends. What is it, a Dragoon Colt?"

The old man chuckled. "You know your guns, son." With a deceptively casual movement of his arm he drew the weapon. The gun gleamed huge and metallic in his fist, seeming to dwarf him with its size. But he handled it with familiar ease. "Forty-four Colt Walker Dragoon," Isaac said proudly. "Not many of them around anymore."

"Not many of them made in the first place," Tom added. The big cap-and-ball revolver had been the standard issue sidearm of the United States Cavalry for a time, but had never been mass produced. It was one of the most powerful handguns made.

Isaac hefted it fondly. "I done took this one with me when I left the pony soldiers. Never saw any point in getting anything different." He slid it back into the holster. "That's a nice-looking piece you're carrying. I cleaned it and your Winchester for you when they brought you all in."

"I'm beholding to you." Tom glanced at the battered old

hat perched atop the curly-haired skull. "Buffalo Soldier?" he guessed.

The dark eyes fixed on him. "Yeah, the Indians called us that," Isaac said softly. He smiled slightly in grim remembrance.

Tom was impressed. During the Indian Wars of the last decades, a few select regiments of black soldiers had seen action against Indians throughout the Southwest, earning the respect of white soldiers and the enemy as well. It had been the Indians who had given them the nickname of Buffalo Soldiers. The name had become a byword for courage and fighting skill.

"I fought the Indians, and before that I fought the Confederates," Isaac mused aloud. "Fighting was a way of life to me before I came here. I was an escaped slave when I joined the Union Army. Don't rightly know how old I was. But just a kid. I ended up in the Fifty-fourth Massachusetts." He paused reflectively, as if to gauge Tom's response.

"You were at Fort Wagner?" Tom asked, incredulously.

Isaac gave a slow nod. His eyes shifted out of focus. "We marched up that beach into the teeth of their guns and cannons, and they cut us down. The whole world was fire and death. One man of every two of us died, but it was the fort turned us back, not the Rebs."

Tom swallowed. The near suicidal attack of the 54th against the impenetrable stronghold of Fort Wagner was the fabric of legend. The battle and its aftermath had earned an irrevocable place of honor in military history for the black soldier. Isaac Jacob's teachers had been good indeed. "How'd you end up here?"

Isaac shrugged. "Drifted up here after I left the cavalry. There weren't no more Indians to fight. The Sister was needing a hand to do the chores here, and I just sort of stayed on."

"Being here must feel kind of tame."

Isaac used his forefinger to tip his cavalry hat back slightly.

"I do miss the fighting days sometimes. But I'm old, and mostly this here suits me fine. Every now and then I have to let some drifter know that the mission ain't easy pickings. But that's not too often." He cocked his head and asked, "You really think Tayback's boys will come after him?"

"Hard to say. Might not hurt for us to post a lookout. The Sister said some of the girls could help."

Isaac nodded thoughtfully. "There's a good vantage point up in the cupola. I guess you might like to have a look around, get the lay of things."

"Yeah, I would."

"I'll give you a tour."

Tom noted that the old man moved with greater ease as they left the kitchen and ascended to the top floor. From there a trapdoor in the ceiling of a storeroom led up into the cupola perched atop the building's roof. The interior of the tiny chamber was cold. From the small windows Tom had a commanding view of the landscape in all four directions. He saw only forested hills covered with snow.

"Any settlements hereabouts?" he asked as they descended from the small tower.

"A few folks down the hills a ways," Isaac told him. "Don't amount to much, and they wouldn't be no use if there was trouble. They don't have a telegraph or nothing to send for help."

With Tom in his mackinaw and Isaac in a heavy beaverskin coat, they left the building. The cold struck Tom like a blow. Once again he felt the weakness in his legs.

"You ain't full recovered yet, son," Isaac chided. "Best take it easy."

Tom nodded grimly. "Does the main building have a back door?" he asked.

"Yeah, but it'll be easy to cover."

Isaac led the way down one of the shoveled paths. As he followed, Tom glanced back at the main building. He paused in midstep at his first good view of the mission. Although

aware of the structure's spacious interior, he was unprepared
for the full impact of its size. Wide and tall, it loomed
incongruously against its hill-country setting. A line of gabled windows peered at him from its third floor. One of
them must belong to his room. The lower windows were
unadorned. Smoke rose from the multiple chimneys. The
cupola occupied the very center of the roof.

"Quite a sight, ain't it?" Isaac had taken note of his halt.
"The old building burned a few years back, and they put this
one up to replace it. Used to be a monastery and a boys
school here, too, the sister tells me. But that's all gone now."

Tom followed him on to the stable where the mules were
housed. Paint and the other horses had been accommodated
there.

"Rubbed them all down," Isaac told him. "You had them
sweating. Didn't want any of them take a chill, but you
couldn't have made it much further."

Tom was beginning to understand a little better the trust
Sister Mary Agnes placed in her caretaker. The milk cows
and chickens were housed in a lean-to off the stable. From
there, Isaac led him to a barn that served double duty as
storage space for hay and as a general-purpose workshop,
complete with a blacksmith's forge and billows. Isaac had
apparently been interrupted in the process of repairing the
metal rim of a wagon wheel. Tom promised himself silently
to give the old man a hand with any outstanding chores
before he left the mission.

A small log cabin served as Isaac's quarters. The spartan
interior was clean and tidy. Tom noted the old trapdoor
Springfield carbine mounted over the fireplace. He guessed
that it also dated back to Isaac's days as a Buffalo Soldier.

The bitter wind of the days before had died, Tom noted as
they left the cabin. It would make traveling in these hills a
mite easier.

"What do you think about the place?" Isaac asked, once
they were back in the main building.

Tom knew the old soldier wasn't asking what he thought of the mission grounds as a homestead site. "If it comes to defense against any kind of a force, we write off the outbuildings and fight from in here," he answered promptly. "Board up the ground floor except for firing ports, and cover the rear. A rifleman up in that cupola wouldn't hurt if we had the manpower."

Isaac snorted. "You might've made a good solider, son."

A bell began to clang. In moments the corridor seemed to fill with girls of varying ages clad in the same plain style of dress Sharon had worn. Tom had an impression of copper complexions and long black hair done up or in braids. Girlish laughter rose amidst the chatter of voices. He recognized the facial characteristics of several tribes—Seminole, Creek, Chickasaw.

"Nigh onto noon," Isaac confided. "The girls are going to eat lunch."

Tom saw more than one glance cast their way, usually followed by averted faces and stifled giggling. He shifted his booted feet uncomfortably. Blonde hair suddenly flashed like gold amid the dark tresses.

"There you are!" Sharon exclaimed. "I was hoping I'd get to see you!" Her face was radiant. "It's all so exciting! Sister Mary Agnes is really a dear, after all. She's been going over everything with me. She says I can sit in on classes this afternoon and maybe start teaching as soon as tomorrow, if I feel up to it."

Her excitement had added a warm glow to her delicate features. She looked lovely. Tom realized he was gazing dumbly at her, and managed a grin. "I'm glad you got along with the Sister. Sounds as if you'll like it here." He was glad he didn't stumble over any of the words.

"Oh, I'm sure I will." She turned her attention to Isaac. "And you must be Mr. Jacob. I'm so happy to meet you. I'm Sharon Easton."

Beneath the full radiance of her smile even Isaac's aged features seemed to soften. "Isaac is fine for me, miss."

Tom grinned at Isaac and said, "Mr. Jacob's been showing me around."

"Well, it's time for lunch," she said to Tom. "Come on to the dining room and eat with us. I'm sure it's all right."

He started to accept, although he wasn't in the least hungry. He hesitated and glanced at Isaac.

"Mostly I takes my meals in the kitchen, miss," Isaac offered.

"Nonsense, Isaac. You know very well you are welcome to join us at our meals." Sister Mary Agnes had appeared from among the bustling schoolgirls. "You, also, Mr. Langston."

"I guess we'd be honored, Sister," Tom said immediately.

"Very well. Come along." Sister Mary Agnes turned briskly away. Sharon flashed a parting smile and hurried in her wake.

"Don't like to eat with all them young girls," Isaac said softly to Tom. "Makes me plumb nervous." He shot Tom a reproachful look. "Just cause you're moonstruck by that pretty little yellow-haired gal ain't no reason to drag me along when you're sparking."

"You acted kind of moonstruck there, yourself," Tom returned.

Isaac laughed and fell into step at Tom's side.

But the noon meal afforded Tom little opportunity to visit with Sharon. She was too busy paying attention to Sister Mary Agnes. Only occasionally would he manage to catch her eye and get a quick smile in return from across the table. Isaac kept his gaze lowered as he ate. He said little.

Tom found himself glancing about the large room with its rough-hewn wooden tables crowded with Indian girls. Their voices rose in a subdued murmur. Tom guessed the sisters would brook little in the way of misbehavior at mealtimes.

Apparently certain of the older girls took turns being responsible for the cooking, while younger girls served their classmates on a rotating basis. This much Tom gleaned from overhearing Sister Mary Agnes explaining procedures to Sharon. He wondered how long their supplies would hold out if they were snowbound for an extended period.

"I take it Isaac has shown you around the grounds, Mr. Langston," the headmistress said to him.

"Yes, ma'am. You have a nice place here."

"The Lord provides," she murmured. "I shall want to visit with you both later today concerning any decisions you have reached." She smiled briefly to close the conversation, then turned her attention back to Sharon.

Young Sister Lenora appeared as they were leaving the dining room in the midst of the girls returning to class.

"The marshal is awake," she told Tom brightly. "He's doing so much better. He wants to see you. I tried to get him to wait until he was stronger, but he was so insistent I decided I better come find you."

"I'll go see him right now," Tom promised.

"Oh, good. Tell him I'll check in on him between classes." Sister Lenora scurried away in the flow of girls.

"You want to come meet the marshal?" Tom asked Isaac.

"Naw, you go ahead. I'll look him up later. I got some things to check on, seeing as how we might be expecting visitors."

Tom headed for the infirmary. He grinned some as he pictured Stever's reactions upon awakening. He could imagine the marshal's bewilderment and frustration upon finding himself an invalid in a girls school.

Stever was sitting propped against the headboard of his bed when Tom entered his sickroom. The lawman peered sourly at him. His slate eyes were dull.

"What in tarnation am I doing here, Langston?" he demanded. "How's the girl?"

"She's fine."

"Where's Tayback? I woke up and found some little nun fussing over me and trying to calm me down by telling me a wild story about us showing up here in the middle of a snowstorm."

"There's some truth in it, I reckon," Tom drawled. "Tayback's locked up safe in the cellar. You were too weak, and the weather was too bad to bring you anywhere but here. If we'd stayed at that cabin, you'd have died, for certain." He used his boot toe to hook a chair over to him. Reversing it, he straddled the seat and rested his arms on its back. "And that little nun most likely saved your life."

Stever snorted. "The last I remember is going out to fetch the gal's horse. After that I don't recollect much of anything. What do you mean, the nun's story is true?"

"If you'd hush for a minute, I'd tell you."

"Well, go ahead. Tell me." Stever glared with some of his old fire.

Tom propped his chin on his crossed arms. "Well, it's like this," he began. Concisely he related the events following Stever's collapse, their journey here, and the conditions they had found.

"You hauled me and Tayback to a girls school?" Stever interrupted.

"I told you, we didn't have no choice. Sharon helped out or we wouldn't have made it. Now shut up and listen."

Stever maintained a surly silence while Tom finished. Then he shook his head. "You whipped Tayback in a fistfight?" he asked skeptically.

"That seems to surprise everybody," Tom said. "My pa taught me some about that kind of fighting."

"Your pa again?" Stever scowled. "Just who in blazes was your pa, anyway?"

"You ever hear of Carter Langston?"

Stever's jaw dropped. "The Texas Ranger? You're his kid?"

"So he always claimed."

"By the heavens. I guess maybe you would be a fair-to-middling hand in a fight, if he taught you. Even the other Rangers say he was the best. He still alive?"

"Died a few years back in a gunfight with five owlhoots."

"What happened to them?"

Tom met his gaze levelly. "They're all in prison or dead."

"You have anything to do with that?"

Tom looked away. "A little." He felt Stever's eyes on him.

The marshal didn't pursue the matter. "You say Tayback's locked up in the cellar?"

"Yeah. He won't get loose. Me and the caretaker are checking in on him every so often."

"I guess I better see to things, just the same." Stever pushed his bedclothes away and made as if to swing his legs off the bed. Then he grimaced and went shockingly pale.

"Lay back down, you durn fool!" Tom snapped.

Panting a little, Stever settled back to his former position. He said something under his breath. "You're certain he can't get free?" he asked then. At Tom's nod, he continued. "Who's this caretaker you mentioned?"

"An old black man. An ex-slave, among other things."

"Great," Stever said bitterly. "And he's helping keep an eye on Tayback?"

"He might surprise you some," Tom suggested.

Stever disregarded the comment. "Has Tayback said anything?"

"Just boasted that his men will find him, and tried to get me to turn him loose."

"You didn't listen to him?" Stever demanded with sudden intensity.

Tom shrugged. "He's still locked up in the cellar." He studied the lawman for a moment. "He seems awful confident his men will come looking for him. Think there's much chance of it?"

Stever sagged back against the headboard. "I don't know," he admitted wearily. "Normally I wouldn't think much of the ability of a man the likes of Tayback to command loyalty from his gang. But he's got a Yaqui halfbreed who rides with him. Calls him his Segundo. I never heard any other name for him, but he's as mean as a locoed rattler. In his own way, he's almost as bad as Tayback, except he's cold mean—doesn't feel a thing. Tayback enjoys hurting and killing. And for some reason that halfbreed's loyal as a dog to Tayback. With Tayback a prisoner, Segundo will be running things. There's no telling what he'll do."

Tom recalled Tayback's cryptic reference to his second-in-command. "This Segundo—how would I know him if I was to see him?"

"Lean, dark, face like a hawk. No lips to speak of. Looks all dried out. Sounds like a Mexican when he speaks English." Stever fell broodingly silent, then tilted his head quizzically. "Can the caretaker here handle a gun?"

"I'd say so," Tom answered dryly.

"You would, huh? Well, that makes three of us—you, me, and him—if trouble comes."

"You ain't in any shape to fight."

"I can pull a trigger!" Stever's tone was fierce.

"We're going to post lookouts. The headmistress volunteered some of the older girls to help out."

"I don't cotton to having a bunch of Indian girls and an old man looking after my prisoner," Stever growled.

"You don't have much choice."

Stever's face twisted with sudden pain. He sat up and shot out a clawed hand to grip Tom's arm where it rested on the chair back. "Look after things, Langston," he gritted. "I got to count on you until I get back on my feet. You understand?"

Tom nodded tightly. "I understand."

Stever's face went even paler. His taloned fingers fell away from Tom's arm. He flopped back on the bed and lay still, save for the ragged rise and fall of his chest.

CHAPTER 6

"VERY well, gentlemen," Sister Mary Agnes said to Tom and Isaac. "I am leaving these matters in your hands. However, I do want to be apprised of your plans."

"Yes, ma'am," Tom said.

"Yes, Sister," Isaac said, his reply merging with that of Tom.

Sister Mary Agnes smiled, and the austere lines of her face softened. "Sister Lenora tells me the marshal is much improved. I have led the girls in prayer for him at the beginning of each class today."

Tom had left Stever in a fitful sleep and gone in search of Isaac. A tall slender girl with clear eyes set in her high-cheekboned face had found him first, and escorted him to the office of the headmistress. Isaac was already there. Seated at her desk, the Sister had listened to them carefully.

"Is a guard to be kept on Mr. Tayback?" she asked when they were finished.

"We figured one of us would check on him every hour," Tom answered. "Keep the girls away from the cellar. Isaac and me will be responsible for taking his meals to him and looking after him."

"I have selected several girls to assist you in keeping watch. Their function, however, is to be confined to maintaining a lookout from the cupola. They are not to handle guns."

Tom and Isaac nodded acceptance of the condition.

"I appreciate both of you gentlemen," she went on with quiet sincerity. "I feel quite comfortable in placing our safety in your hands."

Tom muttered a polite acknowledgment and tried not to shuffle his boots.

Sister Mary Agnes picked up a small bell from her desk and rang it peremptorily. In moments the tall Indian girl who had been Tom's guide appeared. Tom guessed her age at seventeen or eighteen. She curtsied politely to Tom and Isaac.

"Yes, Sister?" she inquired of Mary Agnes. Her eyes seemed to glow with respect and admiration.

"Gentlemen, this is Fawn. She has almost finished her studies here and is considering going back East for further education if funding can be obtained. She will be in charge of the girls who are to assist you. I have already gone over the matter with her. Fawn, gather the other girls in the dining room to receive instructions from Isaac and Mr. Langston."

"Yes, Sister." She glanced shyly at Tom and Isaac before hurrying out.

"Please let me know if you need anything else, gentlemen." Mary Agnes dismissed them with a smile.

Tom felt some of his earlier weakness return unexpectedly as they left her presence. Isaac glanced at him shrewdly. "You go rest awhile, son," he advised gruffly. "I'll speak to the young ladies and set them to keeping watch. You still got some recovering to do."

Tom didn't argue. The journey and his fight with Tayback had been a grueling ordeal. He expected to feel the effects of it for days. He wondered with admiration at the unquenchable energy Sharon had displayed in being introduced to her new position.

Sprawled drowsily in the small bed in his room, he thought of her smiling face and shining golden hair. Moonstruck, Isaac had called him. He mulled the thought over. He had known Sharon Easton for less than two full days, he realized with a sense of shock. But those days had held a lifetime of peril and challenge. Throughout their trials, she had shown unflagging spirit and courage. A man could do worse than be moonstruck by the likes of Sharon Easton. A man could even build dreams around her.

But she had her own dreams of teaching the Indians—there would be no room for a shiftless cowpoke with only vague notions of someday settling down on a place of his own.

He wasn't sure when he dozed, but he awakened feeling refreshed and much stronger. He took his gear from the wardrobe and shaved.

A look out of the window confirmed to him that it was midafternoon. The snow was no longer falling, but the gray clouds appeared unchanged. There was no trace of sunlight penetrating their layers. The cold beat against him even through the glass.

He had a clear view of the surrounding countryside stretching away in front of the mission. Idly he scanned the scattered clumps of woods thrusting up like islands from the sea of snow. Then he stiffened. Back up in the hills, the bundled figures of three horsemen were picking their careful way through the snow. Unmistakably, they were headed for the mission. Tom squinted but couldn't make out details.

He turned sharply away from the window. Where were the lookouts? The oncoming trio would reach the mission shortly.

He snatched his mackinaw and his Winchester. Opening the door, he almost collided with Fawn.

"There are riders coming, Mr. Langston!" Her soft voice was urgent.

Tom strode down the corridor. Fawn had to hurry to keep up. "Where's Isaac?" he demanded.

"I sent one of the other girls for him."

Tom nodded approval. "You need to alert Sister Mary Agnes."

"I have," she told him.

Tom hefted the Winchester in his fist and increased his

pace. The three riders could be no more than wandering cowhands, he told himself. But a sense of urgency welled up inside of him, just the same.

Isaac was waiting at the massive front doors. He held the carbine Tom had last seen in his cabin. "Three of them," he told Tom. "Riding in from the hills. Not making any effort to hide themselves."

"I saw them," Tom advised tersely.

They turned as Sister Mary Agnes approached. "That will be all, Fawn," she told the hovering girl.

Fawn bobbed her head obediently and retreated. Mary Agnes moved to a window and pulled the curtain aside to peer out. "Now they are passing the barn," she reported.

Tom sensed a foreboding in the nun and the old soldier that matched his own. He went to look out of the window past her shoulder. The three riders had entered one of Isaac's shoveled paths and were walking their mounts boldly up to the front of the mission.

He could see more of them now. Their coats were ratty. The edges of rags protruded from their sleeves and collars where they had been stuffed to provide further insulation. All of them had sheathed saddle guns. Their faces were wrapped against the cold, but their hands were bare. They almost looked like holdup men, he reflected grimly.

"I shall go out and speak to them." Sister Mary Agnes left her post at the window and swirled a cape about her shoulders. "Isaac, please accompany me. Mr. Langston, I think it best if you remain out of sight."

Tom nodded agreement. The less these strangers knew of outsiders at the mission, the better.

Sister Mary Agnes waited until one of the men shouted a rough greeting. Immediately she swung open the door and stepped out to confront them. Isaac was close on her heels. He shifted sideways a little to be clear of her as they faced the strangers.

From the window Tom could see the riders clearly. He

crouched with his Winchester at ready. He could use its barrel to smash the glass as part of the same motion of bringing it to his shoulder to fire, he calculated automatically. The voices carried to him muffled by the cold and the glass.

"We're mighty glad to see you, Sister." The foremost rider pulled down his bandanna to speak, revealing a fleshy stubbled face, red from the cold. "We been caught out in this weather for nigh onto two days now. We'd sure admire a place to shelter and some vittles to fill our bellies."

The three of them had spread out in a line facing Isaac and the headmistress. Tom studied them carefully. Only the spokesman in the middle of the line had his face uncovered. Tom detected gunbutts bulging under the coats of all three. These strangers were heavily armed. Their bare hands would make it easy for them to reach their guns. Tom focused his attention on the rider farthest to the right. Something in the way the lean man sat his big gray made Tom's fingers tighten instinctively on his Winchester.

"You're welcome to what we can spare in the way of supplies," Sister Mary Agnes replied to the stranger's request. "But we really don't have the facilities for boarders. I'm sorry."

"We wouldn't be no trouble, Sister," the spokesman persisted. "Just want a chance to get in out of the cold."

"It's impossible. I wish we could be of more assistance to you." Sister Mary Agnes was firm. Tom noticed Isaac holding the carbine at port, as if about to present arms to his old cavalry commander.

"What about the barn or that cabin yonder?" The rider gestured back over his shoulder. "We could bunk out in them just for tonight. Wouldn't hurt nothing, and we'd be on our way come morning."

Tom could sense the Sister's hesitancy. The request was not unreasonable. It was the sort of request he himself had made upon their arrival the day before. As a devout Christian woman, Sister Mary Agnes would be loath to turn away someone who might genuinely be in need of aid.

"Who are you?" she temporized. "What are your names?"

Tom thought the spokesman cut his eyes toward the lean rider on the right as if seeking guidance. "We're just cowpokes, Sister, come into these parts looking for work. Like I told you, we done got trapped in the blizzard. We been without food or shelter for two days now." He leaned earnestly toward her as he spoke.

Isaac turned his head to glance briefly at the headmistress. If she saw the motion, or read anything into it, Tom couldn't tell. Her figure was as rigid and unyielding as a corner fence post.

"You fellows do a lot of roping, do you?" Isaac spoke for the first time. "What with working cattle and all?"

The spokesman shifted in his saddle to look at the old man. His fleshy face twisted in obvious disgust. "You asking us white folks a question, boy?" he sneered. "Ain't you forgetting your place? You ain't been spoke to yet. You shouldn't go talking to your betters without them speaking to you first." His horse shifted nervously beneath him.

"You are welcome to some supplies." Sister Mary Agnes's voice was colder than the frigid air. "Then I'll have to ask you to leave. We can do nothing further for you."

The spokesman licked his thick lips. This time his glance toward the lean dangerous rider was obvious. "Look, Sister." His voice had hardened. "We don't think it's quite right of you and this old slave to be turning us away into the weather like you're doing. It just don't seen the Christian thing to do."

"What could you possibly know of anything Christian?" The voice of Mary Agnes was laced with scathing contempt.

Some unseen signal seemed to pass between the three riders. There was a tensing of their stances, a kind of tightening of their postures.

This had gone far enough, Tom thought. Violence bristled

among the three strangers. His concealed presence was no longer an advantage. He reached the door in two strides, pulling his mackinaw about him as he moved. He stepped out into the cold.

The strangers reacted with startlement at his appearance. He moved to the far side of Mary Agnes so that he and Isaac bracketed her. It put him almost directly in front of the lean rider.

Significant glances were exchanged among the riders. The spokesman and his companion were clearly looking to the third man for guidance.

"Who are you, stranger?" the spokesman demanded then.

"A servant of the Lord," Tom answered coldly. "You heard the Sister. We've got nothing here for you. We can't spare any supplies. You aren't welcome here."

"Just a minute, mister—" the spokesman began.

Tom looked deliberately away from him. His eyes locked with dark empty ones in the black-kerchiefed face of the lean rider. "What's your name?" Tom snapped.

The lean man did not react for a moment. When he spoke he had a Spanish accent. "I go by many names."

"Is Segundo one of them?" The Winchester was hard and cold in Tom's grip.

The rider's sinewy left hand rose slowly to the black kerchief across his features and drew it down. The face revealed was one such as Stever had described. His hard eyes gleamed with cold cruelty. "That is not a name, señor."

"Just yours, maybe." Tom was apprehensively aware of the bulk of the horse and rider towering above him and of the harsh nervous scent of the animal in his nostrils.

Slowly the rider shook his head. His eyes did not seem to move. "Not mine, señor," he said softly. "I know of no one who goes by such a name."

Peripherally, Tom could glimpse Sister Mary Agnes's face set in firm resolution. His attention was on the lean man, alert for any sudden movement. He was the dangerous one of the trio. Isaac could account for the other two if guns came into play.

The lean rider was gauging him as well. The lipless mouth lifted in a heartless grin. "I think you and the old black man do not belong here in a house of God," he said in his soft tones. "I think you are men of blood and death, and you should leave this nun and her squaws to the hands of God."

"Men of blood and death," Tom echoed. "Such as yourselves, Segundo?" The movement of his head took in all three riders.

The lean man didn't disavow the name. With a deliberate movement that could not be misinterpreted, he lifted his left hand and drew the kerchief once more up over his face. The evil smile vanished behind the black fabric. Only the dark eyes peered at Tom unchanged. "For your help." The sibilant tones were muffled. "¡*Gracias!*"

"*De nada.*" Tom's lips barely moved.

With that same deliberation of movement, the rider turned his horse away. His companions followed him as he guided the animal back the way they had come. They passed the outbuildings and disappeared into the trees.

For the first time Tom became aware of the cold. It touched his face with icy fingers, and he realized he had been sweating. The empty eyes of the lean rider had done that to him.

"Let's go inside now." The Sister's features were pinched, maybe from the cold, and maybe from strain.

Once inside, with the heavy doors shut behind them, she spoke again. "They weren't cowboys, were they?" It was almost a statement.

Isaac shook his grizzled head. "No, Sister. Them weren't cowpokes."

"How do you know?"

"Their hands," Isaac explained quietly. "They weren't wearing no gloves. A gunsel or an outlaw does that if he wants to be able to get to his gun real fast. And there weren't no callouses on their hands. A real cowboy, he'll have callouses from using a rope and working a fenceline, like Tom's hands there."

Tom knotted his fingers into fists then straightened them. The cold of the rider's eyes wouldn't leave him.

"They weren't cowpokes," Isaac finished. "If Tom hadn't come out, we might've had trouble."

"Were they Mr. Tayback's men?"

"I think the man I called Segundo is his second-in-command," Tom told her. He had no business concealing anything from her under these grim circumstances.

"Is that all of them?"

"I don't expect so."

"Do you think they will return?"

"If they think we've got their chief, they'll be back."

"Very well, gentlemen. I shall be in prayer." She turned and left them.

"I'll go up to check with the young lady on watch," Isaac said. "No need telling the marshal at this point. He don't need to be upset in his condition."

Tom nodded agreement. "I'll look in on Tayback."

He descended to the basement and left his Winchester and mackinaw outside Tayback's cell. The big outlaw shifted awkwardly about the floor in the uncertain light of the lantern.

"Turn me loose, cowdog," he grunted.

"I'll turn you loose in a jail cell," Tom promised. He advanced a step until he loomed over the shackled outlaw. The handcuffs were still secure, he saw.

"You look worried, cowdog." Tayback was squinting up at him. "Something riding you?"

"You're the one should be worried," Tom retorted.

"Not me." Tayback showed his teeth. His grin had an edge to it in the dim light, as if at any instant he might spread his lips wider to reveal gleaming fangs. "I ain't got a care in the world." He cocked his head, and his eyes shone with a cunning glow. "Any of my boys showed up yet? I reckon they've had about enough time to cut our trail and follow us here. How about it, cowdog? Is that what's riding you?"

Tom studied him. Could Tayback somehow know? It was impossible of course, but some of the cold from outside seemed suddenly to have filtered into the makeshift cell. "A backshooter like you couldn't find very many men who cared if you lived or stretched a rope," he said deliberately.

Tayback sneered. "I got plenty to bust me out of here."

"How many's that?" Tom prodded casually.

"You'll find out when they come. You better have them nuns start praying."

"I'll have them pray for you."

He saw the big man's eyes shrink and harden as they had before. Something evil surged up from their depths. He stepped deftly clear as Tayback hurled himself across the floor with an inhuman snarl. Crablike, Tayback scuttled after him. Tom retreated another step, then was out the door as a groping hand snatched at his ankle. He banged the door shut, and heard Tayback's fingers claw like talons at the wood on the other side.

Tom hurried from the cellar.

CHAPTER 7

"THERE can be little doubt that these men were members of Mr. Tayback's disreputable band," Sister Mary Agnes said. "Further, Isaac and Mr. Langston are of the opinion that they will return."

Sharon Easton listened with rising apprehension as the headmistress spoke. She struggled to keep her face composed. Sister Ruth was seated at her left, and Sister Lenora on her right. Sharon resisted the urge to sneak glances at the two nuns and, instead, kept her eyes on the headmistress.

Her frantic thoughts tumbled over one another like pebbles rolling down a hill, dislodging others as they went, until a landslide of fear threatened to crash down on her rationality. And on an even deeper level she felt a dim sense of dismay that her fears were not for the Indian girls, nor even for herself, so much as they were for Tom Langston.

He had faced the outlaws with Isaac and the Sister. He had been in danger, and when—if—the outlaws returned, he would undoubtedly be in danger again. He would insist on placing himself in the forefront of risk to protect the school and its occupants. She recalled the horror of witnessing his brutal fight with Tayback. She had been unable to do more than stand by helplessly. Now, he would be facing terrible hazard again.

"For the time being, we shall say nothing of this to the students. I have already instructed Fawn and the older girls on this point." Sister Mary Agnes was studying each of them in turn. She spoke with firm deliberation. Sharon wondered if the headmistress had read any of the fear plunging through her mind. She made an effort to concentrate on the older woman's words.

"Our routine shall continue as usual. If possible, I want no variation from it. I have placed Isaac and Mr. Langston in charge of our defense. We will obey their orders in the event of a crisis."

Sister Mary Agnes paused. Her calm handling of the situation was reassuring. Now Sharon did glance at the other two nuns. Sister Ruth's open face was pale, and Sister Lenora's customary gaiety had vanished. But in them both Sharon could sense a spirit of steely resolve.

"Naturally, I expect the highest standards of behavior from all of you, such as are customary to those of our calling as teachers."

Sharon realized the headmistress had looked directly at her as she had spoken. Of course. As a novice teacher, her conduct would be most in question. She forced her heart back down her throat. "Yes, ma'am," she said in a voice that was gratifyingly steady.

A flicker of what might've been approval passed in the eyes of the headmistress. For the first time during the meeting she relaxed slightly in the wooden swivel chair behind her desk. Her mouth softened. "We may be alarmed without due cause," she admitted. "But I would rather take these precautions than be caught unprepared should trouble come." She surveyed her audience for a moment. "Do any of you have questions or anything to contribute?"

"Sister?" Sharon heard her own voice say.

"Yes, Miss Easton?"

"I can help Tom—Mr. Langston—and Isaac if need be. I mean, I can help defend the mission—" She broke off awkwardly at the unreadable expression on the Sister's face.

"Certainly, we are all willing to do whatever is necessary." The Sister's mouth softened again. "But thank you for your offer. Is there anything else? Very well. Return to your duties. I will keep you advised."

Dismissed, Sharon left the office with the other two teachers. She had been sitting in on Sister Lenora's class when a flustered Ruth had arrived to summon them both to the staff meeting. Now Sharon looked inquiringly at the younger nun.

Sister Lenora hesitated. She seemed to read something in Sharon's face. She smiled suddenly. "It's almost time for the mid-class break," she said. "I'll go back and dismiss them. There's no need for you to come. Meet me back at the classroom in a quarter hour."

Wondering how much of her motivation Lenora had discerned, Sharon hurried away. Where would she find Tom?

Other than the frustrating lunch when she had been unable to talk with him, she had not seen him since their joint meeting with Sister Mary Agnes that morning. After spending almost forty-eight uninterrupted hours in his presence, the separation from him seemed unbearably hard.

She knew so little about him, she realized. She did know that he was brave and compassionate. The rigors of their journey here had established that much. But what of his past? And what of his hopes and dreams? What did he think of her and her own expressed ambition of teaching the Indians? Stargazer and castle-builder, her father had lovingly called her. But he had given in to her desire for an education so she could attain her goal. Was there a place in Tom Langston's dreams for a girl like her?

Her face felt suddenly warm, and she realized she was blushing. Such thoughts were surely improper, she chided herself. But there was warm satisfaction in them, just the same.

She couldn't find him on the ground floor, and she hesitated at the thought of going to his room. Was that too bold? She was still hesitating when one of the heavy front doors opened, and he stepped in out of the cold.

He was wearing his faded mackinaw. His Stetson was pulled low, so his lean face was in shadow. He carried his Winchester confidently in one gloved hand. She stifled the impulse to run to him, but her pace was still immodestly faster than a sedate walk.

"Tom!" She was embarrassed at the excitement and relief in her voice.

His mouth widened in a grin of what seemed genuine pleasure as he saw her. He had found time to shave, she noted immediately. He spoke through his grin. "Thought you'd be in class, or helping the Sister or something." He hefted the Winchester with sudden awkwardness, as if unsure what to do with it.

"There's a break during the class." The words came out of her in a breathless rush. Why hadn't she found a looking glass to check her appearance before trying to find him? She probably looked a mess. "I wanted to see if you were all right."

His grin faded completely. "The Sister told you, huh?" he questioned in a glum tone.

She nodded, suddenly aware that she had come very close to him before halting. She stepped back slightly, but was unable to make herself retreat fully to what would've been a proper distance. She felt the warmth of her blush returning. "Three men—outlaws—came and asked questions," she said, condensing Sister Mary Agnes's report. "You and Isaac backed them down."

He tilted his Stetson back with his forefinger and appeared to find something behind her of intense interest. "They weren't really looking for trouble." He hesitated, then added, "Leastways, not yet."

She shivered at the darkness in his voice.

He apparently mistook it as a reaction to the cold. "It's chilly here. Let's get away from the door." He was almost gruff. "I been out checking the boundaries."

"Did you find anything?" She looked up at him as he ushered her further down the corridor.

He shook his head. She thought he was going to add something, but he remained silent. "It should be warmer in here." He let her precede him into the mission's cozy parlor. Once in the room, he leaned his rifle against the wall, then shrugged out of his mackinaw and hung it on a wooden coatstand.

Sharon suddenly worried about whether Sister Mary Agnes would disapprove of them being alone in the parlor together. Gratefully she spied an ancient upright piano in the corner and crossed to it. She seated herself and brushed her fingers over the keys. She was conscious of Tom coming to stand over her. He leaned his lanky frame easily against the piano.

"You play?" he asked.

"A little." She was sure she was still blushing, and so would not look up at him. "We had an old piano at home, and my mother taught me some. Then I learned more at school." She played a few soft notes. Her hands felt clumsy. "Where's your home?" she found the nerve to ask.

She listened without looking up as he spoke fondly of his childhood as the son of a Texas Ranger. When he was done, she finally turned her gaze up at him. "Where are your folks now?"

"They're both dead. Ma died of a fever, and Pa was killed."

"You didn't want to become a Texas Ranger like him?"

His eyes slipped out of focus. Slowly he shook his head. "I thought about it." He appeared to be debating over exactly what to tell her. When he looked back down at her, she sensed that he had made a decision to share some private part of himself. A warm feeling of thankfulness touched her.

"My pa taught me how to fight and track and such," he began. "I think maybe he sort of planned on me following him into the Rangers. He never said much about it, though, except to call me his 'little ranger' when I was just a youngster."

She dared a quick glance at him. His appealing features had softened with memories, but a hardness crept back into them as he continued to speak.

"When some men killed my pa, I took out after them myself. It was something I had to do. I couldn't just stand by while the Rangers tracked them down." Brooding thoughts flickered in his eyes. "I used everything my pa had taught me, and I found them, one by one. Those that would surrender, I took in alive. The others I brought back over their saddles."

He paused for a long reflective moment. "The Rangers called me a hero. They tried their best to get me to enlist."

"And you didn't?" she urged gently.

He shook his head. "I wanted nothing more of manhunting and killing. I know how to use my gun and my fists and a few other things, besides. I'll fight if I have to, but I ain't cut out to be no professional fighting man."

"What did you do?"

He hitched his shoulders in a shrug. "Drifted up north. Worked at cowboying and some odd jobs. Finally I hired on as a cowhand for Mr. Dayler. He's a fair man, and that sort of work suits me as well as anything, so I've stayed there." Some thought seemed to sadden him, and he fell silent.

Embarrassed suddenly at her own boldness in questioning him so, she ran her fingers over the keys in a lilting melody.

He straightened up from where he leaned against the piano. "You best be getting back to class, I expect."

"I know." She pushed the bench back and stood. It put her very close to him for an awkward tantalizing moment.

Then he stepped away, and she retreated around the far end of the bench. "I'll see you at dinner, I reckon," he told her. "Isaac and me are doing some checking on things."

"Be careful!" The words burst from her in an impulsive rush.

He nodded soberly. "You don't worry about things none, okay?"

"I won't," she lied with as much composure as she could manage.

It seemed to make him feel better, just the same. "Maybe

you can really play for me when this is over." He nodded at the piano with a grin.

"I'd like that." She smiled.

As she headed back to the classroom, she met Sister Mary Agnes in the corridor.

"Class will be beginning soon, Miss Easton. Do not be late."

"I was just going to the classroom now." She all but stumbled over what she said.

Sister Mary Agnes regarded her coolly. Despite her words, she seemed in no hurry to discontinue their encounter. "Your first day here has been a hectic one, I fear. I trust the future will be of a more pacific nature."

"Yes, I hope so, too. But I already feel at home. Sister Ruth and Sister Lenora have been just dears to me." She realized she was almost babbling and tried to cut off the flow of words. Had the headmistress seen her and Tom emerging from the parlor? Had their innocent meeting offended the Sister's sense of propriety?

The older woman's expression seemed to confirm her fears. "I have been here at Sacred Heart for over five years now, Miss Easton. During that time, I have seen and endured many things. I have watched members of my flock die of pestilence while I was unable to help, and I have been near death myself from the same cause. I have faced hostility from the families of some of the girls who have chosen, of their own volition, to come here to learn. I have seen young women, whom I loved as my own, reject this school and all that it stands for, despite my best efforts and prayers. There have been times when we were short on food, and other times when Isaac and myself have faced men much like those who came today."

"Yes, ma'am," Sharon mumbled inadequately.

"I tell you this, Miss Easton, to impress upon you the fact that Sacred Heart is a demanding and jealous mistress. She will require of you both commitment and sacrifice."

"I know that, Sister." Sharon kept her voice soft, but she was aware of a defensive note in her tone.

"I hope you do, Miss Easton," Mary Agnes went on firmly. "And I hope you remember it in setting your own personal priorities. You know that you cannot serve two masters."

"We both serve the same Master, Sister, and it's possible to serve in many ways. No one is limited to only one type of service."

Sister Mary Agnes inclined her head slightly to one side as if to view her from a new perspective. Sharon's heart was thundering in her breast, but she forced herself to meet the older woman's gaze levelly.

"You have wisdom beyond your years and your experience, Miss Easton," she conceded at last.

"Thank you, Sister." Sharon lowered her eyes in polite acknowledgment.

"I hope that your wisdom will guide you in choosing the ways in which you serve."

Was there a wry note to the Sister's comment? Sharon kept her eyes downcast. "I'll do my best, ma'am. I promise you that. Sacred Heart is very important to me."

"Very well, Miss Easton. I can ask nothing more of anyone, including myself. And now, unless I am greatly mistaken, it is I who have made you late to class. Sister Lenora is no doubt expecting you at this moment."

"Yes, Sister." Sharon slipped past her.

"Oh, and Miss Easton?"

Sharon turned. "Yes?"

"Mr. Langston is a good man."

Sharon felt her eyes widen. "I believe he is, too," she stammered.

Unexpectedly Mary Agnes smiled with a warmth that brightened the hallway. "God bless you both," she said softly.

"Thank you, Sister," Sharon managed, but the older woman had already turned briskly away. Only the warmth of her smile seemed to linger.

Her thoughts a bewildered whirl, Sharon headed for the classroom. Sister Lenora had just called the class to order when Sharon arrived. She settled into her seat near the back of the room to observe the proceedings.

Her mind wandered as Lenora labored over English grammar with the twelve girls in the class. This was the last session for the afternoon. Her first day at the mission had, indeed, been a hectic one. She felt tiredness edging in on her mind and body.

The door to the classroom opened with unnerving suddenness. Sister Ruth rushed in. Her face was even paler than it had been earlier in the office of the headmistress. She spoke in whispered tones to Lenora.

The younger nun faced her students. "Class is dismissed for today." Her face had also grown pale. "You will return to the dormitory and remain there until further notice."

Sharon hurried up to the two nuns as the students filed obediently out. "What is it? What's happened?" she demanded.

"The outlaws have come back," Sister Lenora told her soberly. "This time it is the whole gang."

CHAPTER 8

THEY came riding brazenly down out of the hills in the gray light of late afternoon—fifteen hard-eyed men armed for battle. Passing the outbuildings, they drove their horses on through the snow, converging on the front doors of the mission.

Tom eyed them grimly through the viewing portal. He spotted Segundo riding in the vanguard. Tayback had been right: his gang had come to get him out, and there were plenty of them to do the job.

He drew back from the portal and donned his outdoor gear. He left his hands bare. The metal of the Winchester felt cold against his palms.

Where was Isaac? he wondered with a scowl. Tom had not seen him since prior to his brief visit with Sharon in the parlor. There was no time to look for him now.

Once more he peered out at the oncoming riders. They were just halting in front of the mission. Tom noted that they were careful not to pack themselves too closely together. Bunched men made easy targets and tended to interfere with one another when it came to gunplay. These dangerous men weren't making that mistake.

But they were clearly not planning an immediate assault, either. Segundo would want to talk first. He would expect the sheer number of his followers to result in the immediate release of their leader. Tom's jaw tightened.

"*Hola* the mission!" came Segundo's voice.

Tom brushed his hand reflexively over the butt of his Colt. He had pulled up the coattail of the mackinaw so the gun would be easy to reach. He would not cower behind the doors

90

to converse with these backshooters. For the moment they must be confronted openly. To show weakness might draw an immediate attack.

A footstep sounded behind him. "I will go out there with you," Sister Mary Agnes said.

"Not this time, Sister," Tom told her. "Last time those boys came for socializing. This time I reckon it's a little more serious."

Sister Mary Agnes drew herself up rigidly. Angry sparks flashed in her eyes. "I am responsible for this mission and its students. I will not hide or cringe before these pagans!"

Tom grinned slightly. "I guess you and I are a lot alike, Sister," he drawled. "But that ain't no place for you outside. Remember, you put me and Isaac in charge. If you didn't mean that, then I guess now's the time for me to know it."

"You in the mission! Come out! We will talk!" Segundo called.

Slowly some of the rigidity went out of Sister Mary Agnes. "Very well." Her tone was still stiff. "I shall do as you say, until such time as my conscience dictates otherwise. I trust I have not misjudged you, Mr. Langston."

"Say a prayer for me, Sister." Tom levered the Winchester so it was on full cock and ready to fire. He turned and went out the door.

The cold slapped at his bare face. He felt suddenly exposed and vulnerable. Surreptitiously he slid his finger through the guard and over the trigger of the Winchester. He held the rifle across his chest as his eyes raked the mounted men facing him. They had arranged themselves in a rough line. Hard cases and owlhoots to a man, he thought. He saw one long-haired white man with a bow and arrows slung comfortably over his shoulder. They were a rough crew.

"Ah, it is you." Segundo looked down at him from his horse. The half-breed's menacing face was bare to the cold. Beside him was the fleshy spokesman from the earlier visit.

He had a Winchester laid casually across the pommel of his saddle. Like Tom's, it was cocked and ready to fire.

"Where are the others?" Segundo hissed. "The nun and the old man?"

"What do you want?" Tom queried flatly. He could feel the coldness creeping into the knuckles of his fingers. He hoped it would not slow his hands if he had to use the rifle.

"We want to talk," Segundo told him. "But I don't know your name. What do I call you?"

"We've got nothing to talk about," Tom answered coldly.

"Oh, but I think we do." Segundo's voice was silky.

"I'm listening." It was impossible to watch them all. Tom tried to be alert for any sudden movement in their ranks.

"We think a friend of ours is here," Segundo explained. "His name is Tayback. We believe you hold him prisoner."

"This is a school, not a prison."

Segundo's smile was cold and humorless. "Nevertheless, we believe Señor Ned is here," he persisted.

"Go look somewhere else."

Segundo spread his palms out. "There is nowhere else. We have followed the trail of the man who took Señor Ned prisoner. I believe he is a marshal of the United States. He was wounded and may not be alive. We followed the trail to the old cabin. After the storm we found it again—four horses, one of them Señor Ned's, another pulling a travois, probably bearing a wounded man. The trail led here." Segundo shrugged expressively. "So, you see, there is nowhere else."

"We can't help you. Sorry."

"I think you do not want to help. And that is a foolish thing."

Tom hitched his shoulders in answer. "Now we've talked. Go on and leave."

Segundo looked deliberately at the men to either side of him. "There are many of us, and only you. Yet, you give us orders. It is a thing I do not understand."

"It's nothing you need to understand." He was running a greenhorn's bluff, Tom knew. But he had no other hand to play.

"If we want to," Segundo said carefully, "we will look for Señor Ned."

"No," Tom replied bluntly. "I don't think you will."

Segundo cocked his head like a lizard on a rock and regarded Tom with puzzled eyes. "You are stubborn," he commented. "Why don't you simply turn him over to us, and we will ride out?"

"Will you?" Tom countered with open skepticism. The halfbreed was a worthy second-in-command for Tayback, he thought.

"How will you stop us if we decide to look?" he asked curiously.

"I'll stop *you*," Tom told him. "That's all you have to worry about."

"No," Segundo corrected. "I must worry about Señor Ned. I will not rest until I find him."

"You won't find him here."

"I think I will look." Segundo kicked one foot free of its stirrup.

"Don't get off that horse!" Tom's command locked him in place.

The former spokesman at Segundo's side snapped his Winchester from the pommel of his saddle. Tom caught the movement. He had an instant's view of the barrel coming in line with his chest. Faster, he shifted his own Winchester and pulled the trigger. The rifleman reeled backward out of his saddle. The convulsive skyward blast of his rifle merged with the tail end of Tom's shot.

Tom tried to swing his Winchester to bear on Segundo, levering it as he did. He knew he was out of hope. They had called his bluff. He had no chance in an open gunfight against this many men. They would cut him down in a hail of bullets.

Another shot cracked through the winter air from behind the outlaws. It froze their hands as they grasped at their weapons.

"Just sit pretty and you'll live, boys!" a familiar voice commanded.

Tom saw the sturdy figure of Isaac Jacob in the doorway of the barn. The ex-Buffalo Soldier held his smoking Dragoon Colt in his right fist. His carbine he wielded one-handed in his left.

Heads were turning to stare at the apparition. Segundo did not look around for the source of the shot. His revolver was half clear of leather when he saw Tom's rifle cover him. He aborted the draw and darted a quick glance over his shoulder.

"You're first," Tom growled. "Whatever else happens, you go down."

Some of the tension eased out of the halfbreed's lean figure. He let the revolver slide back into its holster.

"No sudden moves!" Isaac called. "I'm old, and my eyesight ain't so good. I'll just kill the first man I see move, and not take no chances."

He advanced a step out of the barn. His weapons seemed to cover the whole band of outlaws. "Nice and easy, boys," he warned, and moved still closer.

Tom saw glances being cast at Segundo. They weren't going to buck a crossfire without his lead.

He grinned at Tom almost mockingly. Slowly he spread his palms once again. "Perhaps we will meet another time," he suggested.

"Take him and get out of here." Tom nodded at the man he had shot. He couldn't tell whether the fellow was dead or alive.

Segundo jerked his head, and two of the riders dismounted to heft the limp form across his saddle. Tom knew then.

The halfbreed paid his subordinates no mind. He stared

hard at Tom from narrow eyes. "You would do well to turn Señor Ned loose," he said softly.

"Everybody wants to give me advice," Tom said. "Now I'll give you some. Forget about Señor Ned. He's out of your hands. Leave here and don't come back."

Segundo flashed a cold reptilian grin in reply. He backed his horse carefully until he could see that his men had gotten their downed companion draped across his saddle. Then he shot one last glance at Tom, wheeled his horse about, and led his men through the snow, back up into the hills.

Only when the last of them had disappeared did Tom back toward the mission, keeping his eyes on the hills. A bush-whacker might still offer a threat.

Isaac joined him just outside the door. He ceased his own scanning of the hills to bare his teeth in a quick grin at the younger man. "I almost didn't make the party."

"You could've waited a little longer to see if I was able to outshoot all of them," Tom said sardonically.

Isaac chuckled. Side by side, they paused a moment, surveying the woods where the outlaws had vanished. Tom wondered if hostile eyes were fixed on them from the under-brush there.

"I think you done killed the one you shot," Isaac said.

"I think so, too," Tom replied tightly. He remembered the limp body slung over the saddle. There had been no avoiding the killing, he knew, but he didn't take pleasure in it.

"At least that's one less to worry about," Isaac mused. "I could've picked off another one, I guess, but I shot high to warn them. Maybe I'm getting soft in my old age."

Tom shook his head. "My pa always told me the only time to kill a man is when you haven't got any other choice. You ain't no backshooter."

"I think I would've liked your pa."

"Yeah," Tom agreed. "How'd you end up out in the barn, anyway?"

"I was just out prowling when I seen them coming," Isaac

explained. "You was back in the mission, and I knew you'd come out to face them. So I figured it would do us good to have them in a crossfire. Worried me a bit that you might let the Sister come out, though."

"She wanted to." Tom shook his head. "She don't take orders very well."

Isaac laughed, then grew sober. "You think that was all of them?"

Tom nodded. "I expect it was." The shadows were long on the hills, he noted. It would be dark soon. "It was enough," he added.

Behind them the door came open slightly. "Is the danger past, gentlemen?" Sister Mary Agnes asked.

"Just stay clear of the door, Sister," Isaac murmured respectfully. "We're coming in."

She stepped back to give them room. Inside, Isaac hefted the stout wooden bar and set it firmly in place. There was a sudden rush of feet, and Sharon almost hurled herself into Tom's arms. She quickly stepped clear.

"Thank God you're all right! I heard shots!" She looked back and forth questioningly between the two men.

"We're fine," Tom managed.

"Miss Easton," Sister Mary Agnes interjected sternly, "your place is with the students."

Sharon retreated a pace and bowed her head contritely. "Yes, Sister." Tom felt a pang for her.

"I will apprise you and the other teachers of what has happened here, shortly. In the meantime, rest assured, I will call on you if your assistance is needed."

"Yes, ma'am," Sharon responded. Tom had the impression that she wanted to look at him, but dared not beneath the Sister's eye. She turned away. Her departing footsteps were rapid.

Sister Mary Agnes cut a sharp eye at Tom. For a moment he had the ridiculous feeling that she was going to ask him what his intentions were toward Sharon.

Then her expression softened. She let her gaze take in Isaac as well. "Thank you, gentlemen," she said formally. "You both risked your lives."

Tom felt his face burn. "They were Tayback's men, all right, Sister." His voice was gruffer than he had intended.

"Did they say anything of significance?" she inquired. "I could not hear all of the conversation."

"If we turn him loose, they promise to leave us alone," Tom told her.

"Do you believe them?" she demanded immediately.

"Not enough to risk cutting Tayback free," Tom said without hesitation.

"And you, Isaac? What do you think?" she addressed the old man.

Isaac shifted his feet. "Shoot, Sister, you can't put no stock in the word of the likes of outriders like them. We go turning Tayback loose, there'll just be one more of them to deal with, and him the leader, to boot. As it is, holding him prisoner here might just give us an edge. Could be, they won't want to push things so fast if they think their boss might get hurt in the ruckus."

Mary Agnes nodded as if his words confirmed her own analysis. "I am going to go explain the situation to the teachers and the students," she announced. "They have a right to know what has transpired."

Isaac waited until she was out of earshot. "Come dark," he warned, "they'll be back."

"I know," Tom agreed, broodingly. "I reckon she does, too."

CHAPTER 9

"BY thunder, I ain't no invalid!" Stever raged. "Help me up from here, Langston! I heard shots. Tell me what's going on, you hear?"

The bearded lawman was sitting on the edge of his bed. He had swung his feet to the floor. His good left arm was extended to grip the bedpost. The sweat of exhaustion gleamed on his bare torso, and pain squinted his slate eyes almost shut. His bandage stood out starkly against his skin.

Tom didn't move from the doorway where he leaned. "Lay back down and I'll fill you in," he said.

"Blast you!" The muscles in Stever's arm flexed. On trembling legs he forced himself upright and glared defiantly at Tom. "There! I'm up!"

"Let go of that bedpost, and you'll fall down." Tom kept his voice cold. "You ain't in any shape to be on your feet, much less trying to fight."

In Stever's condition, Tom knew, being up and about just might kill him. The strength he had shown at the cabin had been dissipated by his wound and his illness. He waited while the lawman fought a silent struggle. Stever would have to find out for himself what his limits were.

With a despairing sigh, the lawman sank back down at last. The power and anger seemed to drain out of him at once. "What happened out there, Langston?" he asked weakly.

Tom told him, beginning with the earlier visit of the three outlaws, then describing the return of the entire gang and the gunplay that had resulted.

Stever sagged still further as he listened. He lifted his head when Tom finished. "You're sure it was Segundo?"

"It was him."

"And that was the whole gang, too," Stever mused. "The one you shot sounds like Mac McCarthy. He was a no-good horse thief and gunman."

So now his victim had a name. Tom doubted he would forget it.

"You know they're coming back," Stever went on. "When it's dark, Segundo will have his best woodsmen try to sneak up on this place. He's got two or three who could do it."

"Isaac and me will be watching for them," Tom promised.

"That old black man came to see me." Stever grunted and added grudgingly, "I guess he'll do to cover your back."

"He saved my hide out there."

Stever's slate eyes fixed on him. "The two of you still ain't enough. Not to stand off Segundo and the rest of Tayback's pack."

"We're all there is," Tom reminded. "And they've lost one man already."

Stever glared about the room in exasperation and bemoaned, "It was a tinhorn's move to bring Tayback here, Langston."

Tom didn't answer. He regarded the lawman steadily.

At last Stever swung his legs up onto the bed. The effort brought a grimace to his face. Gingerly he laid his head back on the pillow. "Tell me how you're planning to defend this place."

He listened, his eyelids drooping almost shut, as Tom spoke. Occasionally his eyes opened fully and he made a suggestion. "Sounds like you've got it covered about as well as possible," he admitted finally. "By thunder, I wish I could lend a hand, though. But I'm weak as the runt of the litter."

"The building's like a fort," Tom told him. "We can hold it." He put as much confidence as he could into his voice. But even a fort needed enough defenders to do the job, he thought dismally.

The rustle of material behind him made him turn. Sister

Lenora drew up sharply as she saw him. Her pretty features were set in an intense expression beneath her cowl.

"Oh, Mr. Langston! I was just coming to check on the marshal."

Tom stepped aside to let her pass. He saw her figure stiffen as she took in Stever's sprawled form.

"I knew it." She hurried to the bed. "I knew you'd hear those gunshots and get all upset. Just look at you, out from under the covers, and all worn out!" Determinedly she began to tuck the covers in around the lawman. He scowled murderously, but didn't resist.

"You just can't go fretting about things, or you won't ever get well," she chided as she worked. "Sister Mary Agnes told us that Isaac and Mr. Langston here had matters well in hand, so there's no need of you worrying about anything."

Stever looked past her at Tom. "Keep an eye on things," he ordered. "I'll be up to helping later tonight."

Tom turned away from Sister Lenora's vehement protestations of the prophecy. He felt a grim empathy for Stever, trapped and helpless while other men defended him and his prisoner.

He found Isaac in the cupola, gazing out at the pale vista of snow below. The early darkness of winter had fallen, but the whiteness of the snow made objects stand out to the skilled eye. The hills and the woods were a blacker mass in the gloom. Isaac had broken out one of the small windows, allowing the cold air from outside to invade the small chamber. He crouched with the barrel of his carbine propped on the window ledge. His grizzled head turned slowly back and forth as he surveyed the terrain in front of the mission.

"I got the back door barred so a mule couldn't kick it down," he advised Tom. "The rear windows on the ground floor are up high, so I figure we're pretty secure from that quarter for now."

Tom murmured a wordless response. Fragments of Stever's words kept flicking through his mind.

"How's the marshal?" Isaac asked.

Tom pulled himself out of his musings. "All het up because he can't lend a hand."

"Figures." Isaac didn't cease his methodical scrutiny of the mission grounds. "I stopped in and had a visit with him earlier. I reckon he'd stand his ground when the lead starts flying." He shook his head sadly. "A man like that needs to be able to fight for himself, not have to be looking to others to do the job for him."

"He can't even stand up on his own, much less fight."

"I know, but it's still a bad thing when a man can't help fight his own battles." A reflective note touched Isaac's voice. "I recollect when I was a kid joining the Yanks to fight the Rebs. It felt mighty good to be taking a hand in fighting for freedom.

"I didn't even have me a name to give them when I signed up—leastways, not a proper one." His voice seemed to come across a great distance. "I'd just been called Joe-Boy by my owners for as long as I could remember. Didn't have no name other than that. I never knew my pappy. Never even knew who he was. And they sold me away from my mammy when I wasn't knee-high to a hound dog. Children were cheaper to buy than adults, and a child could be made to do a man's work for a while, if it didn't kill him." He paused for a dragging beat of time. "Don't remember what my mammy used to call me. So I was just Joe-Boy until I took out and joined the Yankees. When they said I had to have a real name, I picked two out of the Good Book and told them I was Isaac Jacob. Looking back, I guess that was what I fought for much as anything—just being able to have my own name."

"It's a good name," Tom said.

Abruptly Isaac stiffened. He peered out at the terrain below with deadly concentration. After a moment he relaxed.

"Something out there?" Tom asked. He could see nothing.

"Coyote, maybe." Isaac was terse. "Gone now. But those boys will be coming for us. You mark my words." He swiveled his head around and gazed at Tom. "You figure to stay up here?"

"Just wanted to get a look at the terrain at night from up high," Tom answered. "I figure a few of them will try sneaking up on us before they mount any kind of major attack."

Isaac grunted agreement. Tom could not read his expression in the gloom. "What you planning to do?" the old man asked.

"I reckon I'll go out and meet them," Tom said.

For a moment longer Isaac studied him. "You played that kind of game before, son?" he demanded. "Stalking a man at night in the woods is some different from facing his gun in a shootout."

"I've played it."

"All right." Isaac didn't push the matter. "It ain't a bad idea. I might've tried it myself thirty years ago. I'll be up here covering you as best I can. Maybe between us, we can give them some grief."

"Right." Tom eased down out of the cupola.

Back in his quarters he donned his heavy leather chaps, then sorted through his gear until his hand closed on the worn hilt. He drew out the sheathed hunting knife and bared its keen blade. It wasn't the giant bowie knife his father had favored for this sort of work, but Tom had never been a knife man. There were cleaner ways to kill. But a blade was silent, and outside in the night, silence might mean the difference between life and death. The hunting knife wasn't a bowie, but it could do the job if he had nothing else.

Bundled and armed, he moved through the corridors. He left his Winchester behind. It would only get in his way.

Sister Mary Agnes emerged from her office as he passed. She eyed him without expression. "You're going out after them," she stated finally.

Tom nodded. "They'll be coming soon. I'll be there to

meet them. It's best this way, Sister. I'll need someone to bar the door behind me, and then let me back in."

"Very well. I have given orders for the building to be kept dark. No lights are to be shown near windows. Isaac warned me of the danger of snipers. I shall be waiting at the door for your return."

Tom slipped silently out of the mission and heard her bar the door after him. He paused in the shadows and felt the cold begin to tighten its numbing grip on him. He was glad he had not encountered anyone else beyond the headmistress in the halls of the mission. Sharon's apprehensive features flashed in his mind. She would not want him to be doing this. Resolutely, he put the thought aside. Distractions, like noise, could get him killed.

He had one more stop to make. He reached the barn without incident, staying to the shadows where he could. The stark whiteness of the snow reflected what little light there was, and made night vision easier. He guessed Isaac had spotted him from his vantage point in the cupola. He hoped the old soldier wouldn't mistake him for one of the enemy.

In the barn he moved mostly by feel. But on his earlier tour with Isaac he had seen the item he sought, and it had not been moved. He bared his teeth in satisfaction as his hand closed on the handle of the hatchet. He hefted its weight—not so different from the hand axes used by some of the old Apaches down in Texas, and on which his pa had trained him. It made a welcome addition to his armory.

Back outside he paused in the shelter of the barn's looming height. The mission was a great darkened silhouette against the snow. He saw no lights within it and remembered Sister Mary Agnes's orders to that effect.

He moved to the corner of the barn. The prolonged cold had hardened the snow enough to largely support his weight. He would not have to wade through its two-foot depth as he had yesterday on their trek to the mission.

He gazed up into the blackness of the woods. How many

of his men would Segundo send? Stever had guessed two or three, and so far the lawman's knowledge of the gang and its members had seemed both accurate and thorough. Figure at least three of them, he decided. The front of the mission was the obvious target, but Segundo was canny. Despite Isaac's confidence that the back was secure, the halfbreed would likely have at least one of his men approach from that quarter. Isaac's attention had been centered on the area in front of the main building. That left the rear vulnerable.

Using the outbuildings and then the woodline for cover, Tom circled wide around the grounds. He moved cautiously, refusing to hurry. He probed the night with his senses. Somewhere around him, he was sure, were other human predators on the prowl.

From the edge of the trees he surveyed the rear of the mission. The ground floor windows were up high, as Isaac had said, and there were only a few widely spaced windows on the upper floors. Anyone approaching the building would have to cross an open strip of about seventy-five feet with only a few saplings for cover. An interloper would be exposed there, but so would anyone trying to silence him from up close.

Tom crouched behind a fallen tree and watched and calculated. Once an owl glided through the trees overhead like a lost spirit. Tom shivered and wished the mackinaw were thicker. He strained his ears against the eerie silence. Far off, a lonely wolf howled at the cloudy sky.

From higher back up in the trees another sound came whispering to him at last. Tom held his breath. Faintly he detected the crunch of snow beneath carefully placed feet. Animal or human? he wondered. He waited tensely. Another sound filtered to him. He recognized it immediately as the unavoidable rubbing of fabric against undergrowth. Someone was moving up there in the night.

Whoever it was knew how to navigate through the brush at night with a minimum of noise. And if he kept his present course, he would emerge from the woods about thirty yards from Tom's place of concealment. If Tom waited until then to make his move, they would both be caught in the open. He needed to strike, if possible, before his prey left the cover of the trees.

Tom eased back from his hiding place. Although the interloper might detect Tom's movement just as Tom had heard his, it was unlikely that whoever was out there was expecting to be stalked. This gave Tom an edge, if he could make use of it.

Tom began to work his way parallel to the tree line. The snow gave a little beneath each step, and the undergrowth reached out with entangling clawing fingers. He was hoping to intercept his prey before the fellow emerged into the open, but he could not move with any great speed unless he wished to give away his own presence. Frequently he paused to listen and keep track of his enemy's position.

The distance separating them narrowed. As yet, Tom had not seen the other man, but he realized that unless he increased his pace, his quarry would be out in the open before he reached him. He had no wish to try closing with the fellow without the benefit of cover.

Tom moved faster. He felt as though he passed through a ghostly netherworld of eerie beings with fleshless, groping limbs. He was sweating now, even in the cold. His dampness made the air even colder on his face.

Unexpectedly he felt his foot break through the snow almost to the top of his boots. His full weight came down on a dead limb buried from sight. It gave with a muffled snap. Tom went rigid. He could hear nothing. The outlaw must've stopped also, alerted by the sound of the breaking branch.

Tom waited, not daring to draw breath. His heart pounded louder and louder until it seemed to deafen him.

Finally he detected the faint sounds of his enemy's movements once again. Undoubtedly satisfied that the breaking branch had been caused by a wild animal or a heavy load of snow snapping a limb, the fellow was moving on toward the mission. Tom ghosted forward, breathing shallowly to lessen the sound of his breath. He gripped the short hatchet in one gloved fist.

He saw his prey at last. A piece of the night seemed to have been given human form. Tom could make out the silhouette of a Stetson above a bulky coated figure. The outlaw carried some sort of rifle in one hand, and he moved with a feline stealth.

A shot would bring him down, but it would also alert any other of his compadres in the area. This was work for the hatchet or the knife. Tom waited, standing motionless.

The fellow paused as if some sense of danger had touched him. He was ten feet away—too far to be sure of a successful rush, Tom calculated. He willed himself to total stillness.

Slowly the Stetsoned head turned in Tom's direction. Tom could imagine the man straining to pierce the darkness with his eyes. Tom knew that if his quarry was visible to him, then he, in turn, would be visible to his enemy, although it might take the fellow a moment to identify his form as being human. Tom had no choices left—he hurled himself forward in a rush. The yielding snow made his steps clumsy. He heard his quarry's grunt of surprise.

The outlaw tried to bring his rifle into play. Its awkward length was too great for hand-to-hand fighting. It got in his way.

Tom swung the hatchet, using the blunt end. He felt it glance off the outlaw's skull, knocking his hat awry. The outlaw staggered beneath the impact. Tom reversed his stroke and swung again, backhanded. This time the blunt end of the blade struck solid. The outlaw collapsed to the snow.

Tom stood over him, waiting and watching. The brief struggle had been virtually silent, and he had detected no other stalkers. He let a couple of minutes slide past. Satisfied, he knelt and checked the fallen man. The fellow was alive and should survive if his companions found him in time. But he would not be taking part in combat any time soon. He offered no further danger to the mission.

Tom straightened fully erect. Abruptly, the sound of a shot cracked from the direction of the mission.

Isaac Jacob blinked and gave his head a brief shake of disgust. Tom had disappeared only moments ago, and already he was seeing things. His eyesight wasn't what it had been twenty years ago, and the patterns of shadow on the pale expanse of snow played tricks on his vision. Had he really seen motion there beneath the trees? Had something moved in the black cover of the shadows?

He swept his gaze fully across the terrain, then refocused his eyes on the suspect area. Was anything different? There was a danger in what he was doing, he knew. If he concentrated too hard on one spot, he might well miss significant movement from another quarter. For the first time, the full weight and restrictions of his age seemed to settle on him. He thought of the nuns and students in the building below. He was responsible for them, as well as for the new teacher and the wounded marshal. It was too much responsibility for a tired old black soldier, even with the help of the young cowhand, Tom Langston.

He had lost track of Tom after he left the mission and went to the barn. The young man moved like an Indian scout. Isaac had expected nothing less, but not knowing where Tom was meant there was some risk Isaac might mistake him for one of the outlaws in the darkness.

He watched and waited, and finally something moved. He was certain this time. It was near the same spot he had noted before. His eyes had not been playing tricks on him.

He lined the familiar barrel of the old carbine on the thicket at the edge of the woods. A shadow shifted in the darkness there. His finger curled around the carbine's trigger. But it was still too early to fire. Whatever lurked down there might be no more than a fox or a coyote, although he knew in his gut that it was not.

The shadow gained form and substance. It became the shape of a man moving forward in a crouch. He paused at the edge of the woods. Isaac eased up on the trigger. Still too soon, he mused. Let the intruder come even further into the open.

Isaac swallowed a bitterness in his mouth. He had no taste for shooting a man like this, with no warning or chance. But there was no choice.

The crouching figure moved clear of the underbrush. Isaac pulled the trigger. The carbine flashed and roared. The figure seemed to jerk backward and vanish in the thicket. At the same instant Isaac's eye caught a wicked flash from further back up the hill. Simultaneous with it, a bullet crashed through the small window beside his head. He ducked low. His fingers moved automatically to cock the carbine and reload it.

Like a military strategist, he realized numbly, Segundo had stationed a rifleman to cover the mission while his woodsmen worked their way close under cover of darkness. Isaac shifted sideways on his knees. He straightened, jammed the barrel of the carbine out the newly shattered window, and fired at the point where he had glimpsed the muzzle flash. Instantly he ducked back. He had no real hope of managing a hit with the carbine under these conditions, but if he could come even nearly as close to the sharpshooter as the man had come to him, he would be satisfied.

Another shot ricocheted off the bricks of the cupola. He heard a third strike solidly and embed itself. Whoever the sharpshooter was, he had a repeating rifle, and he was good with it.

For the moment Isaac didn't return the fire. Instead, he edged his head up until he could peer over the window frame. In the darkness he stood no danger of silhouetting himself, but the sniper was far too deadly for him to take risks, just the same. He could detect no sign of movement from the thicket. His first shot, he sensed, had gone true.

He scanned the terrain with practiced eyes, and let the seconds crawl by. Motion flickered. A hunched figure moved at an awkward lope toward the woods. A second invader was retreating from the unexpected resistance. He had managed to get close to the mission itself.

Isaac started to line the carbine. A six-gun went off once, twice, three times from the corner of the building. Instantly Isaac swung the carbine back to the hillside and fired at the sharpshooter's position. The six-gun had belonged to Tom. He must've spotted the fleeing outlaw and tried to bring him down. The muzzle flashes would give the sniper another target. The threat of the carbine just might dissuade the unseen rifleman from firing. Isaac could only hope that Tom would realize what was happening and take cover.

The loping figure disappeared unhit. No muzzle flash showed from the far hillside. The clamorous ringing in Isaac's ears from the gunshots was the only sound. He continued to watch alertly.

One more of them down, he figured. He couldn't count on the off chance he had managed to hit the sharpshooter. He wondered how Tom had done. He guessed that the outlaws would give it up for the night. They had lost at least two of their men.

"Isaac!" a muffled voice called from beneath his feet.

He grimaced as he recognized Sister Mary Agnes's voice. Of course, she would be concerned for his safety. He should've figured some way to let her know he was all right. She must've hurried up here once the gunfire ceased.

He lifted the trapdoor. The austere face of Sister Mary Agnes peered up at him in the light of an uplifted lantern.

"I'm fine, Sister, just fine," he assured her before she could speak. He felt a pang of unworthiness at the look of relief that softened her features momentarily. "Lower the lantern a little bit, Sister. That's better—don't want no light up here. What about the boy?"

"Mr. Langston? He is not hurt. He returned and reported that he had encountered one outlaw behind the mission. He would say little more about the matter. I left him with Miss Easton. She insisted on seeing to him."

That made three, Isaac totaled grimly. And it meant he had made a dangerous miscalculation. He hadn't believed any of them would approach from the rear of the building, offering as it did, no easy access. Thankfully, Tom had figured otherwise. The realization made him feel older than ever.

"You're certain you're all right, Isaac?" Concern was evident in Mary Agnes's voice.

"I'm fine, ma'am. Just a little cold maybe. If one of the girls could bring me some coffee, it'd go nice."

"Of course, I'll see to it myself." She hesitated. "You'll be remaining up there, then?"

"For a little while, Sister," he told her. "I expect I better."

CHAPTER 10

"OH, Tom, you could've been killed going out alone in the night with those murderers out there. Please don't take a chance like that again," Sharon said, laying her hand on his arm.

She was seated beside him in the parlor. The room had no windows, so the single oil lamp did not cast silhouettes that a lurking sharpshooter might target.

Tom gazed at Sharon's lovely features in the warm glow of the flickering flame. He had trouble finding words.

"I had to do it," he offered lamely. "We might not have been able to spot them from inside until it was too late. And this isn't over. Those men may come back. I'll have to do whatever needs to be done to protect this place, if that happens."

She drew her hand back from his arm. "I know. But just be careful."

"I'm always careful."

She winced and turned her face sharply away. Tom realized his curt reply had stung her. "I'm sorry," he said awkwardly. "It means a lot that you care what happens to me. It gives me more reason to be careful."

She lifted her face, and he saw the glint of moisture in her eyes. "I do care what happens to you," she whispered. "And it frightened me when I learned you had gone out there alone. What happened?"

"They were trying to sneak up on the building. I knocked one of them out."

"There was shooting, too."

"That was Isaac. He got another one with his carbine, then

traded some shots with a rifleman up in the hills. There was a third one on the grounds who got spooked when the shooting started. I took some shots at him, but he got away." Tom remembered seeing the fleeing figure disappear into the brush. His hand had been cold, or he might've brought the outlaw down.

The coldness still had not left him completely. Sister Mary Agnes had met him at the door as he returned from his foray. She had listened without comment as he reported. Sharon appeared as he finished.

Sister Mary Agnes nodded curtly to the younger woman. "See to Mr. Langston, Miss Easton. I must go check on Isaac." She had turned abruptly away and left them there.

Sharon had helped him out of his mackinaw. It was nice to have her fussing over him, but he saw distress touch her face darkly as she noted the knife and hatchet in his belt. She ushered him into the parlor then left to return shortly with a cup and a pot of steaming coffee. Tom drank gratefully and felt the liquid begin to take the edge off the cold that had seeped into his veins.

Now he picked up his cup from the coffee table and sipped at it again. It bothered him to realize he had placed Sharon and the whole Sacred Heart Mission in danger by bringing Tayback here.

"What's wrong?" Sharon asked unexpectedly. He felt her discerning eyes on him. "Your face grew all dark and grim."

"Nothing." He put the cup back on the table. "The Sister will probably be back shortly."

"I know, but it's all right for us to talk for a few more minutes. You heard her tell me to tend to you." A faint spark of mischief danced in her eyes. "She likes you, you know."

"Couldn't prove it by nothing I've seen," Tom said in surprise. "I figure she'd be happy to be rid of me right now, if it could be arranged."

"That's not true!" Sharon protested. "She told me you

were a good man." She paused briefly, then added, "But I already knew that."

Some of his gloomy mood seemed to infect her as well. She laid her hand once more on his arm. "Tom, you know I can help. I told you that I know how to use a gun."

"Maybe it won't come to that," he forced himself to say. "They might've had enough after tonight." He wished he could believe his own words.

"If only we hadn't brought that awful man here." She sighed.

The words cut him like the blade of the hatchet. Stever had called his decision to bring Tayback here a tinhorn's move. The outlaw's presence would draw the lightning down on Sacred Heart. And Tom himself was to blame. He had as good as condemned to death the nuns, the students, Isaac, and Sharon by meddling in the marshal's affairs.

"You best see to the girls," he said, remotely.

Sharon nodded sadly. "I will."

He got to his feet. For a moment longer she remained seated, gazing wordlessly down at her folded hands. Then she rose slowly. They were very close. He could smell the sweet scent of her. Abruptly she shivered, as if a cold wind had rushed over her. She lifted her face, and he saw that it had gone pale. Tears misted her eyes once more.

"I'm scared, Tom," she whispered. "I shouldn't be, but I'm so scared."

He reached out and drew her to him. Her arms closed around him desperately, and he mustered all the resolve he could.

"We're still alive," he told her. "Don't give up yet."

She clung to him, then her arms loosened as she disentangled herself and drew back. "Where's my faith?" she murmured.

"Go on," he urged softly. "See to the girls. Try not to fret."

"Oh, I need to take these back to the kitchen." Her eyes had fallen on the coffeepot and cup. The small domestic chore seemed to hearten her. She placed the dishes on their tray, then straightened with it in her hands. She gave him a firm smile. "I'm better now," she assured him. "I won't give up, I promise."

Tom swallowed hard and forced a grin. She turned away and swiftly left the room.

He collected his gear and went cautiously down through the caverns of the building.

At the door to Tayback's cell, Tom lit the lantern. The keys to the handcuffs were with the key to the storeroom door. Tom pocketed them, then opened the door and lifted the lantern to light the interior of the cell.

"Ha! I figured you'd be coming for me, cowdog." Tayback grunted. "I heard them shots. My boys are here, ain't they?" Triumph gleamed wickedly across his face.

"They've come and gone," Tom told him flatly. "They left three of their number behind who won't be robbing no more banks or holding up any more stagecoaches."

"But you're here for me, anyway, ain't you? You've seen the light. You come to turn me loose before my boys come back. I'm going free!"

"You ain't going nowhere except to jail," Tom said coldly. "I'm taking you to Konowa and turning you over to the sheriff there."

"What?" Tayback burst out. "You're loco!"

"I been called worse." Tom set the lantern carefully out of reach. He palmed his Colt and let Tayback get a good look down its barrel. "Stay still so I can reach the cuffs," he ordered. "Try anything and you'll never live to see Konowa."

Glaring, Tayback obeyed. One-handed, Tom undid the cuffs. Tayback eased his leg straight with a sigh of relief. Tom rose and stepped clear. The outlaw's boots and coat were outside the storeroom. He donned them under Tom's gun. Tom handcuffed his hands in front of him, and urged him on toward the door.

"You'll never make it, you crazy fool," Tayback growled back over his shoulder as they moved through the cellar.

"We'll see. Now get going. And keep quiet."

Tayback was obediently silent as Tom escorted him up the stairs. They encountered no one, even as they slipped out of the front door.

Tom was careful to leave the portals locked behind him. It was all he could do. There was no way to bar them from the outside. He found himself wondering where Isaac was. They had seen no sign of the old soldier.

The horses and mules stirred uncertainly as they entered the stable. Tom located Paint and Tayback's big roan. They were in the same stall. He worked quickly to saddle the animals.

He was almost done with the chore when a quiet voice spoke from the doorway. "What in the world you got it in your head to do, son?"

Tayback grunted in surprise, but Tom had somehow been expecting the intrusion. He had doubted all along he would be able to get past Isaac Jacob. The old man drifted forward out of the gloom. He carried his carbine casually under one arm. Tom couldn't read any expression on his weathered features.

"I'm fixing to take him to Konowa and let the sheriff have him," he replied simply.

Isaac gazed up at him for a moment. "I figured it might be some such fool thing," he mused aloud. "I was still up in the cupola, and I seen you bringing him out here. What's got into you, son?"

"If I take him out of here, then maybe Segundo and the rest will leave the mission alone," Tom explained feverishly. "It's our best bet. Come morning, when Segundo shows up, you can tell him what I've done."

Isaac shook his head ruefully. "Might be you're right. But it's a dang fool notion, just the same."

Tom didn't answer. He turned stiffly back to saddling the horses. He could feel Isaac's brooding presence behind him.

"I can't let you do it, son," the old man said softly. "You're fixing to get yourself killed, most likely. You think those boys out there are just going to let you ride to Konowa, big as life, and not lift a hand to stop you?"

"Maybe I can slip past them in the dark." Tom left off his work, and turned once more to face him. "I have to do it." He made his words deliberate. "You ain't going to be able to stop me."

"Don't rightly know about that," Isaac drawled. He appeared to loom suddenly larger.

"Either way it breaks," Tom said carefully, "what have you gained if we tangle?"

"Likely one or both of us hurt," Isaac admitted.

"Likely."

"Wouldn't be nobody to look after the Sister and the girls if them outlaws decided to cause trouble." Isaac was staring at Tom as he spoke.

"You're needed here," Tom pressed. "You can't risk getting hurt bucking me."

Isaac shook his head again. "I still don't like it, son."

"I don't either. But I don't see much choice. Do you?"

Isaac was silent for a moment, then said, "The Sister's going to be powerful angry when she finds out."

"I'm doing it for her and everyone else in the mission," Tom pointed out.

"Oh, she'll understand that," Isaac conceded. "But she won't like you putting yourself to risk."

"We're all at risk as long as he's here." Tom gestured angrily at Tayback.

Isaac's shoulders sagged in resignation. He seemed to shrink in size. "I suppose I got to admit you're right."

Tom felt some of the tension drain out of him. His voice was still tight. "Tell the Sister that if I make it, I'll be back."

Isaac nodded as if the matter went without saying. "She the only one you got a message for?" he asked shrewdly.

Tom thought longingly of Sharon. "If I come back, I'll tell her myself," he responded hoarsely. "If I don't make it, then I guess it doesn't matter, does it?"

"Could be that it does," Isaac objected gently.

"Ain't this all real sweet?" Tayback's crude interjection cut off further talk. "But if you boys was smart, you'd just turn me loose right now and forget this here nonsense."

Isaac glanced at Tayback and said, "I reckon he needs to be gagged."

"I reckon," Tom agreed.

"Don't guess you'd mind if I had the pleasure?" Isaac asked.

"Be my guest." Tom pulled the Colt and used it to gesture expansively. Then he leveled it casually at the prisoner. "Stand tight, Tayback."

"Don't you put your filthy black hands on me, you old—" The rest of Tayback's protests were stifled into a gurgling mumble as Isaac jammed a wadded piece of rag full into his mouth. He used the outlaw's own kerchief to tie it in place.

"There," he said with satisfaction as he stepped back. "That's a real improvement, I'd say."

"Help me get him on the horse," Tom said to Isaac.

Afterward, they tied Tayback's feet to his stirrups to be sure he couldn't dismount. Tom added one last restraint. He dropped the loop of his lariat over Tayback's head and tugged it firm, then snubbed the rope around his saddle-horn. If Tayback tried to break away, he would choke himself.

Tayback glared hatred at him.

From horseback, Tom looked down at Isaac's somber face. "Be seeing you," he said.

"Yeah," Isaac responded. His tone, Tom thought, did not sound at all confident.

"Sister?"

Mary Agnes lifted her head. It had been bowed over her clasped hands for so long that her neck gave a surprising little twinge of protest at the movement. She had left the door to her study ajar as she prayed.

"Yes, Fawn?" she inquired gently.

Hesitantly the girl pulled the door wider.

"Come in," the Sister urged.

Fawn stepped cautiously into the dim room. She drew up suddenly as she saw the kneeling position of the headmistress. "Oh! I'm sorry, Sister. I didn't mean to intrude."

"It's quite all right, dear."

Mary Agnes rose to her feet, rather more stiffly than she would've liked. She seated herself at her desk and smiled at Fawn to reassure her. It was rare for students to be allowed to enter here in her third-floor study. The room was a sanctuary to her from the myriad pressures of running the mission.

Fawn stood almost at attention before her desk. She made a visible effort to marshal her thoughts before she spoke. "I have been thinking and praying over what you told us of these outlaws," she began then. "And I have overheard Isaac and Mr. Langston talk while I was keeping watch."

Sister Mary Agnes opened her mouth to object that she need not worry about the situation. She stopped herself before the words came out. Fawn was not a child. Rather, she was an intelligent, educated young woman. She would have realized by herself just how serious matters were, particularly following the exchange of shots with the outlaws.

"Go on," Mary Agnes prompted her.

"Isaac and Mr. Langston cannot fight that many men alone. They need help."

"It is true they are outnumbered," Mary Agnes conceded carefully. She questioned to herself what conclusion Fawn was leading up to with her analysis. She waited for the girl to continue.

"Neither of them can be spared to attempt to go for help, and the weather is too cold, and the snow too deep for us to expect any assistance to reach here in time." Fawn's voice quickened. "But I grew up on the reservation, Sister. You know that. We had little shelter there. I am used to the snow and the cold. My legs are strong. We walked always on the reservation, since we had no horses." She paused as if to let her points sink in, then plunged on. "I could go get help, Sister! In the darkness, the outlaws would not see me. I could go to Konowa, and have the sheriff send men to help fight the outlaws! Please let me go, Sister!" She broke off further words and waited expectantly.

Sister Mary Agnes felt a thrill in her spirit at the girl's courage. What she proposed—a journey on foot to Konowa—would be hazardous at the best of times. Now, at night, in the snow, with outlaws lurking in the vicinity, the selflessness of her offer was truly inspiring.

"I can't let you do that, Fawn."

"Please, Sister. I would be all right. I would be very careful and quiet."

Slowly Mary Agnes shook her head. "I appreciate your offer, Fawn. I really do. It speaks highly of your character. But you are in my charge here at the mission. I cannot let you expose yourself to such danger." She paused, then added as gently as she could, "And, even if you succeeded in your quest, I'm not sure you would be in time to help us."

"But we've got to do something!" Fawn cried with frustration evident in her voice.

"And we shall, if need be," Mary Agnes countered quietly. "Rest assured on that point, dear. In the meanwhile, you are doing your part by assisting Isaac and Mr. Langston. That is all you can do for now."

Fawn's slender form wilted slightly with obvious resignation. "Very well, Sister." She turned to leave.

"Please wait a moment," Mary Agnes felt compelled to

request. She gestured to the chairs before her desk. "Sit down."

Fawn gave a dispirited smile and obeyed.

"How are the other students taking this?" Mary Agnes asked. It was not a question she would've put to very many of the girls. But Fawn was the oldest, and the Sister respected her intelligence and perception. Further, Fawn had just demonstrated her willingness to assume responsibility.

"A few are frightened," Fawn answered candidly. "But most of them are treating it all like some kind of game."

Sister Mary Agnes had deliberately minimized the danger when she had explained the situation to the students.

"And you?" she asked Fawn softly.

"I'm all right, Sister." She met the gaze of the older woman. "But I know it is not a game."

"No, it's not a game," she agreed quietly. "But we are not without hope. Isaac and Mr. Langston are both very capable men, and they have some experience in matters of this nature." She paused, before adding, "It is times like this when faith is important."

"I know, Sister." Fawn's smile had more strength to it now. "You taught me that."

A sudden warmth for the girl suffused Mary Agnes. Her throat was tight, but she managed to keep her voice composed. "I know I can rely on you, Fawn. And I appreciate you coming here and offering to help. You're a very brave and compassionate young woman."

Fawn dropped her eyes in embarrassment. "Thank you, Sister."

"No, I am the one to thank you, Fawn."

A footstep sounded in the corridor outside. Mary Agnes recognized the grizzled silhouette of Isaac in the doorway.

"I'll be going, Sister." Fawn rose to her feet and slipped quickly out of the room.

Isaac stepped aside to let her pass, then entered the study. "Excuse me, Sister. Didn't mean to interrupt nothing."

"It's perfectly all right," Mary Agnes assured him. "We were finished with our talk."

He halted in front of her desk. His old cavalry hat was almost wadded in his fists.

"Yes, Isaac?" she prompted with a touch of foreboding.

"Well, Sister, Tom—that is, Mr. Langston—took the prisoner with him and left."

"He did what?" Mary Agnes burst out.

She listened with mounting horror as Isaac related his tidings. "When was this?" she demanded when he was finished. At some point she had risen from her chair, but had no memory of having done so.

"Maybe going on a half hour or thereabouts," Isaac answered slowly.

She felt her shoulders drop. It was far too late to stop him. She sank miserably back into her chair. Suddenly, she felt totally helpless.

"The young fool," she said half to herself. "He'll be killed. Why on earth did he do such a thing?"

Isaac wadded his hat uncomfortably. "He sort of blamed himself for putting us all in danger here. He figured this was the only way to make amends and to see to it that we were safe."

"There was no way you could stop him?"

Isaac shrugged.

She recalled the strength of will she had read in the young cowhand, and knew Isaac was right. "Do you think he will be successful in reaching Konowa with his prisoner?"

Isaac was slow to answer. "Don't rightly know about that, either, Sister," he said thoughtfully. "He's good, but he's bucking mighty heavy odds. Might be no one's good enough to do what he's trying to do."

She considered his words. "Do you think the danger for us is over?"

"Can't really count on that." Isaac's answer did not surprise her. "Even if he makes it, and we convince those longriders that Tayback's really gone, there's no telling what they'll do."

"So Tom's sacrifice may have been in vain?"

"We don't know if it is a sacrifice, yet," Isaac pointed out.

"Oh, it's a sacrifice," Mary Agnes assured him. "Whatever happens, it is truly a sacrifice."

Isaac's seamed face grew sullen in thought. "I expect you're right."

"What do you suggest we do in the meantime?"

"We better stay on guard, Sister."

She nodded. "Thank you, Isaac. I will advise the teachers of this matter shortly. I trust I can still leave our defensive measures in your hands." It was not really a question. She knew from experience that her confidence in this old man was not misplaced.

"Yes, ma'am." He accepted the dismissal without protest. "I'll see to it."

She watched as he left. When he was gone, she rose and moved from behind the desk. Her joints were still sore, but that really was unimportant. She knelt, clasped her hands, and began once more to pray.

CHAPTER 11

THEY rode through the darkened woodland. A night wind rattled the bare branches of the trees and cut through Tom's mackinaw like blades of ice. He hunched his shoulders against the cold and did his best to ignore it.

He rode with his Winchester across his pommel. In front of him, connected by the rope, Tayback was little more than a bulky figure in the gloom. With any other prisoner, Tom would have taken the lead. But he was unwilling to trust Tayback behind him, despite the bonds restraining him.

Passage was treacherous through the snow and down the icy slopes. Tom used the rope to guide Tayback's progress. He tried to keep them on a westerly course toward Konowa. It wasn't easy. The snow and darkness concealed landmarks and distorted his sense of direction. He couldn't see the stars to navigate by; they were invisible behind the low-hanging clouds. The world consisted of darkness and trees and snow.

He rode with every sense alert. He sniffed the breeze for the scent of woodsmoke. He strained his ears for the sound of human voices. His eyes shifted constantly in search of movement.

He smelled only the scent of their own horses, heard only the crunch of their hooves in the frozen snow, and saw only the shapes of the looming trees.

He focused out of the corners of his eyes, where night vision was best. He did not know where his enemies might lurk. Segundo would have some or all of them on watch or patrol. If they had a campfire at all, it would be far back from the mission, where its flame would not present a target.

The hour was past midnight, and some of the outlaws were

probably asleep in whatever served as their camp. If nothing else, they would at least have tents to provide shelter from the cold. Tom hoped he and his prisoner would not ride blindly upon them in the darkness.

By now Isaac Jacob would've reported to Sister Mary Agnes what he had done.

What about Sharon? he wondered. Had she been told? He remembered her fears for his safety. Was she fretting even now over his absence and his possible fate? And just how much could he read into her interest? Did it go beyond the concern of a caring friend?

He did not have the right to say anything to her about his own feelings until this whole mess with Tayback was settled. He had told Isaac he would speak to her himself when he returned.

If he returned, the thought came to him as chilling as the cold. He had allowed his mind to wander as they rode. Emotion, exhaustion, and the cold itself were attacking him, gnawing away at his resources of strength and will.

The rope tightened against his gloved hand. Tayback had edged his roan down the slope of a draw. Tom urged Paint on to renew the slack between them. The horses did not sink quite as deeply into the snow now that it had hardened in the cold. But he could still feel the tensing of Paint's muscles as the mustang labored over the icy terrain in the roan's wake.

At the bottom of the draw Tayback pulled his roan to a halt. The steep sides of the deep gully offered some sanctuary from the cutting wind and the bitter cold.

"Keep moving," Tom hissed a warning.

Tayback twisted around to look back at him. He jerked his head to motion Tom forward. Tom shifted the Winchester to bring it to bear on Tayback, and stepped Paint closer to the other horse. Tayback lifted his cuffed hands as if to pull his gag free. Tom gestured sharply with the Winchester, and Tayback dropped them back angrily to the saddlehorn.

"What is it?" Tom demanded in a harsh whisper.

Tayback used his head to indicate the draw. His meaning was plain. Clearly he wanted to travel in the shelter of the deep gully. Its course wound away toward the north.

Tom shook his head. He gestured up the slope with the barrel of his rifle. Grudgingly Tayback turned his horse in that direction. Tom let the rope stretch out between them some ten feet or so, then put Paint up the slope after the roan.

So far, Tom was forced to admit to himself, the outlaw chieftan had been a model prisoner. He had offered only token resistance. But Tom knew better than to relax his guard.

He jigged the rope to alter Tayback's direction slightly. Abruptly Tayback jerked his horse to a savage halt. He swiveled about in his saddle. He half lifted his cuffed hands once again.

Tom kicked Paint so the mustang lunged forward. He jabbed the barrel of his Winchester like a lance, halting it just out Tayback's reach. Tom had a sudden vivid remembrance of how it had felt to be gripped and mauled by those powerful arms.

"Move, or I'll leave your carcass here for the spring thaw," he said, quietly but forcefully. He jerked sharply on the rope around Tayback's throat to make his point.

Tayback swung around, face forward in his saddle. He kicked the roan in the direction Tom had indicated. Tom could read the suppressed violence in the rigid set of Tayback's massive shoulders.

Tom glimpsed movement from the corner of his eye and snapped his head around. For a moment the interweaving shadows of wind-tossed branches made the figure of a man rise up out of the gloom like a specter. Instinct swung Tom's Winchester toward it, but the form turned out to be a small bush.

Tom shook his head angrily. The constant strain of herding Tayback had his nerves stretched taut as a hangman's rope. Before long he would actually be shooting at shadows. He shivered from more than the cold and hunched his head down between his shoulders.

Suddenly, a bullet cracked past his face like the weighted tip of a popped bullwhip. If he hadn't ducked his head, the shot would've killed him.

"Yaw!" he yelled like he was herding a wild steer, and pounded his heels against Paint's ribs.

The mustang surged ahead, hooves kicking the snow high. Startled by the shot and the yell, Tayback's roan was also lunging onward. Paint's rush carried him past the bigger horse. Tom felt the rope jerk taut in his hands. He didn't slow down. Tayback could keep up or choke. His life depended on getting clear of the rifleman, but the horses were slowed by the hampering drifts. Every foot of distance and every bit of speed counted, if they were to escape.

Tayback was pulled sharply forward by the strangling rope tightening around his throat. He drove his roan to keep pace with the mustang. Another shot cracked through the night. One-handed, Tom snapped the Winchester out away from him to work the lever and bring it to full cock. Blindly, he thrust it back in the direction of the shot and pulled the trigger. The recoil flung his arm up, and almost toppled him from the heaving saddle beneath him. He clung desperately for a frantic bucking instant, clamping his legs tight around Paint's body. He regained his balance and glimpsed Tayback riding hard next to him. Side by side, they drove their horses through the snow.

Two more shots from the same rifle chased them. Neither came close. Tom knew their shadowy forms would make poor targets amid the trees, and they were pulling clear of the rifleman's effective night range. The fellow had not been positioned particularly close, and he seemed to be alone. Some sort of guard, maybe, who had glimpsed their shapes as they passed, and opened fire. If the gunman had a horse, he had chosen to throw lead rather than mount and give chase.

But evading him was only the first step. His shooting would certainly alert any other outlaws in the vicinity. Tom hauled back slightly on Paint's reins and gave a tug on Tayback's rope. He did not want to run blindly into other members of the outlaw gang. Gradually he slowed their headlong pace.

No more shots came. The rifleman had lost them in the night. Tom finally brought Paint to a stop. Coughing beneath his gag, Tayback halted the roan beside him.

Tom could hear shouts from behind, muffled by the trees and the snow. Another voice answered. There were at least two men back there. Were the other outlaws lurking ahead? Tayback's coughing had changed into what might be laughter. Tom tugged the rope to quieten him.

Cautiously he put Paint forward, keeping his prisoner abreast of him on his left, away from his holstered Colt. He stared ahead into the night, but could detect nothing to alarm him.

Tom slid the Winchester back into its sheath. He had almost dropped the gun and fallen from the saddle trying to use it during their headlong flight. He bunched up his coattail so the butt of his six-gun was easy to hand.

Their horses plodded on through the snow. The sound of their own breathing and the creak of saddle leather seemed loud as thunder to Tom. He could feel Tayback's threatening presence beside him. He worked not to let it weaken his concentration on their surroundings.

Unexpectedly a horse snorted in the darkness before them. Tom drew up gently on Paint's reins. Off to his right, hooves crunched on snow as a horse shifted its weight. A man coughed. Tom turned his head slowly in a full arc. Dimly he could perceive the motionless shapes of mounted men in the woods about them.

His heart seemed to stop. Unknowingly, they had ridden full into the midst of a party of the enemy.

The owlhoots were not on the move. Tom reasoned that they must be waiting for him and his prisoner to pass by their positions. The earlier shots had alerted them to their coming.

Tom offered up a silent prayer. They had not been spotted yet. Maybe they could still slip through the enemy's ranks in the darkness. A single warning sound from Tayback could betray their presence, he knew. He slid his .45 clear of leather and leveled it across his body at the outlaw's bulk. At this range he would not likely miss, no matter what happened. He could tell by Tayback's sudden stiffening in his saddle that he had seen the dull gleam of the revolver.

Tom brushed Paint with his heels. The mustang seemed to sense his rider's tension. As delicately as a cat, Paint started forward. The roan was bigger and less surefooted. But Tayback, under the menacing barrel of the .45, kept the animal quiet as well.

There were at least four mounted outlaws scattered about them in the woods, Tom counted. There could well be more, he knew. He could feel sweat pouring off of him. It made the wind's touch like cold fire.

They had passed the first man now. Tom angled slightly away from the direction where the horse's snort had sounded. He could still see nothing there. He kept his eyes moving, and suddenly was able to make out the ghostly silhouette of a mounted figure to their left.

Tom swallowed hard. If any of these riders looked at just the right angle in their direction, or caught some faint sound of their passage on the wind, their presence would be revealed.

The figure of the rider on their left passed from Tom's range of vision. Had they cleared the ranks of the owlhoots? he questioned silently.

Tayback's booted foot brushed his. He had let his prisoner get too close to him, he realized. Tom kneed Paint sidewise to widen the distance between them. Before the mustang could draw clear, Tayback suddenly stood up in his stirrups, and swung his manacled hands in a great sidewards sweep. They slammed jarringly into Tom's chest and all but swept him from the saddle. He reeled, almost dropping his Colt as he fought to stay mounted. Tayback caught the loop of rope about his neck, yanked it loose, and flung it from him. Then he ripped the gag out of his mouth.

"Here!" he shouted with all his might. "We're over here! Kill this beggar!"

He hauled the roan's head savagely around and pounded his heels into its sides. The big horse surged away.

"Shoot him, boys!" He was still roaring at the top of his voice. "Get him! There he is!" His voice crashed through the woods and bounced back in thunderous echoes.

Tom kicked Paint frantically. Tayback was free. There was no way he could recapture him. Now Tom would be doing good just to stay alive. He could not fight this many men with any hope of emerging the victor.

Shouts answered Tayback. They were frighteningly close. Gunshots crashed through the night. Tom heard bullets strike the branches overhead. The gang had spotted him. He veered off from his course. He could still hear Tayback bellowing curses and orders. He knew the other riders would be hard in pursuit.

Twisting in his saddle, he fired the Colt back at the leaping shadows behind him. Then he sheathed the weapon as he swung Paint off at yet a new angle. A fusillade of shots split the night. He had not really expected to hit anything with his single wild shot, but he hoped they would be lured toward his muzzle flash while he headed in a new direction.

With no warning, the ground seemed to drop away in front of him. Paint had plunged down the sheer slope of a deep wooded draw. Branches whipped past, clawing at Tom's face and clothes. He could see nothing but blackness below, and he seemed to be hurtling headfirst down into it.

He actually felt Paint's hindquarters lift up as his back

hooves lost contact with the slope in the speed of their descent. The horse's usually sure balance was gone—the slope was too steep. In another instant Paint would flip end over end in a headlong roll that would plunge them to the bottom of the draw and likely kill them both.

Tom flung his weight back in the saddle. The different distribution of his bulk drove Paint's hindquarters down. His rear hooves dug into the snow and ice. With an agile twist the mustang caught his balance and gave one last leap down the slope.

They landed on the floor of the draw with bone-rattling force. The impact almost drove Paint to his knees. The mustang struggled upright as Tom clung to the saddle. Bless him, Tom had time to think. Any other horse would've fallen in making the descent.

He understood suddenly that the draw might serve to conceal them from pursuit. He guided Paint forward, weaving him through the brush and scrub oak that choked the draw. Great speed was impossible here, but stealth might serve him better anyway.

From above and behind him came a sudden crashing of limbs. A man's startled cry of terror mingled with a horse's desperate whinny. Then the crashing came to an abrupt halt. At least one of his pursuers had not seen the draw in time. The outlaw's horse had lacked Paint's agility and sureness of foot. Tom wondered if the fellow had survived the fall.

There were shouted questions and replies. Tom thought he heard Tayback's voice again. The outlaw chieftan would be free of the cuffs now. Doubtless one of the gunshots had been used to sever the handcuff chain. Free, and back in command of his men, Tayback would be lusting hot for vengeance.

The draw Tom followed played out at last in a sparsely wooded level area. He drew rein to get his bearings. His flight from the outlaws had left him even further confused and disoriented.

The crackling sounds of horses passing through dense brush reached his ears. Some of his pursuers were still close behind him. He couldn't afford to take too long in choosing his course. He kicked Paint into a rolling lope through the snow. He swung wide, hoping to circle out from in front of them. In the open, Paint could make fairly good time in spite of the snow. But Tom knew he needed to regain the cover of heavier woods before long.

He risked a prolonged look at his backtrail. He could see nothing but the night. He reined Paint over toward a denser stand of trees, keeping him to a lope. Once more he looked to his rear. Paint's startled snort warned him. As he jerked his eyes back forward, two riders burst out of the woods directly in his path.

He tried desperately to haul Paint aside, but the oncoming pair were too close. They had not been expecting to literally ride into their quarry. He heard their startled cries.

Unable to halt, Paint plowed full against the foremost rider's larger horse, which was driven into the third animal. A handgun roared and flamed almost in Tom's face. The lead outlaw had been riding with his gun drawn. The collision had spoiled his shot.

Both horses were going down in a tangle of flailing hooves and tossing heads. Tom kicked his feet free of his stirrups, and hurled himself sideward from the saddle. The other rider wasn't quick enough. Tom heard his heavy grunt of pain as his horse landed partially atop him and drove the breath out of his body.

Tom lunged up onto his feet. The second rider was two yards away. His horse was floundering off balance in the snow. It had managed to stay on its feet. The rider fought the reins to keep it erect. In another moment he would have the animal under control.

Tom lurched forward with high awkward steps. He reached the rider and grabbed his leg with frantic fumbling hands. He yanked the rider's boot out of his stirrup, and heaved upwards. The outlaw gave a startled cry as he was levered out of his saddle.

Tom wanted to get clear of this pair before their yells drew reinforcements down on him. He swung his head about and saw Paint scrambling to his feet. The first rider and his horse were still down. He was pinned beneath the animal.

Tom ran for Paint. The mustang saw him coming and stood rigid. Tom made the saddle in a bound. With no urging, Paint charged into the woods. Tom ducked low to the saddle as the mustang went dodging among the trees. He felt low hanging branches rake at his back. A six-gun was emptied fruitlessly in their wake.

The shouts of the two fallen riders were already being answered by the voices of the party that had been behind him. These hills seemed to be swarming with Tayback's men.

After a hundred yards, Tom slowed Paint to a safer pace that was also less noisy. The mustang's step was sure. He was apparently unhurt from his fall. There was pursuit to their rear, but it sounded like blind pursuit. Not many of Tayback's men would be able to read sign in the dark. Maybe he had evaded them at last, Tom hoped.

Tayback was free now, he thought bitterly. Maybe the outlaw would take his men and leave the area.

"*Cowdog!*"

Tom froze as the bellowed voice rang through the trees from somewhere far back behind him.

"Cowdog, you hear me good." Tayback's voice seemed to roll up out of the black pit of the night. "I'll settle with you one day. But now I'm going back to that mission. I'm going to pull it down on the head of that uppity nun and that marshal. And I'm going to let my boys have them little girls for their squaws! But I'll keep that pretty schoolmarm for myself! You hear me, cowdog? You hear me?"

Tom rode on through the woods. The echoes of Tayback's words were a long time dying.

CHAPTER 12

"YOU'RE worried about Mr. Langston, aren't you, Miss Easton?" the girl's voice asked quietly.

With a start Sharon drew back from the window where she had been peering out into the night. "Fawn! I didn't hear you." The Indian girl had approached with no more sound than drifting fog.

"I'm sorry." She started to turn away, her eyes downcast.

"No, don't be." Sharon protested. But she could not resist one last look out the corridor window.

From it's second-story height, she had a limited view of the ghostly buildings of the mission compound. There was still no sign of life. Dejected, she let the curtain fall and turned back to Fawn with a weak smile.

"I've been praying for his safe return, Miss Easton," the girl offered with obvious sincerity.

"So have I." Sharon hesitated before continuing. "And when it's just us, 'Sharon' is fine."

It was assuredly a breach of some teaching etiquette or ethic, she reprimanded herself without much heat. At this point, she didn't particularly care. After all, she wasn't too many years older than Fawn, and it seemed foolish to have her maintain the formal mode of address under the circumstances.

Ever since Sister Mary Agnes had revealed Tom's rash departure from the mission, she and the other teachers had taken shifts keeping watch over the dormitory. The girls had all been sent to bed, but there had been little hope of them actually sleeping. When Sister Ruth had relieved her as dorm monitor, Sharon left the dormitory to prowl the halls of the

133

mission, pausing to peer hopefully and fearfully from windows she passed.

She felt Fawn's reassuring touch on her shoulder. "I know how it is to worry about the man you love."

"Oh, Fawn, I don't—," she began automatically, then cut the words off. Did she love Tom Langston? Could she possibly have fallen in love so quickly with a relative stranger? "You have a beau?" she heard herself ask Fawn aloud.

The Indian girl nodded rapidly. Even in the gloom, her reserved features seemed to brighten.

"Tell me about him," Sharon requested. She drew the younger woman to a nearby hallway bench. Fawn clearly wanted to share this with her. She was flattered that a student would seek her confidence. And maybe Fawn's words would distract her from the haunting visions in her mind. "Is he of your tribe?"

"Yes. His name is Running Elk. We have known each other since we were children. We used to play together. And always we somehow both knew that when we were older, he would ask for me to be his wife."

"And did he?" Sharon encouraged.

Fawn's face shone with pride. "Yes. He did it in the old traditional way, bringing gifts to my father's lodge. Many young men would not have done so. The old ways are often forgotten or ignored on the reservation."

"Where is he now?"

A shadow dimmed the brightness of Fawn's face. "He has gone back East to go to the white man's school."

"That's what you plan to do, too, isn't it?" Sharon remembered the headmistress describing her prize student.

"That's right. I'll go when I finish my studies here." She gave a soft sigh. "It has made it hard for us, since we have been apart for a long time now. We write each other every week, but I worry about him being so far away, among strange people and things."

"What is he studying?" Sharon had found herself caught up in this tale of childhood romance and adult commitment.

"The law," Fawn answered her. "He wants to become a lawyer and try to use his knowledge and training to help our people here in our homeland. When I am finished with courses here, I will go to the East also and study. I wish to be able to teach the Indian children on our reservations so that they will be able to live with the white man. If we remain isolated, we cannot survive as a people. Running Elk and I will finish our studies at almost the same time. Then we will come back to be married at the mission here."

"Oh, Fawn, that's wonderful!" Sharon cried softly. "Together you'll be able to do so much for your people!"

Fawn nodded shyly. "That is my hope."

"Maybe I can meet Running Elk one day," Sharon said hopefully.

"Yes!" Fawn agreed eagerly. "That would be nice! You would like him, I'm sure."

"I'm sure I would, too."

Fawn already had her dreams in place and was working to achieve them, a remote part of Sharon's mind reflected. She had felt the same way herself only a short time ago, before Tom Langston had ridden into her life. Her desire to help the Indians, her schooling to become qualified as a teacher, and her efforts to win appointment at Sacred Heart had left her little time or desire for romance. Now that she had found it—or, at least, the hope of it—she resented the circumstances that threatened to snatch it from her before it ever had a chance to blossom.

"Is it your time to be on watch?" Sharon forced herself to ask. She wouldn't let her personal feelings interfere with her responsibilities and duties as a staff member here, she vowed.

"No. Songbird is watching now."

"Well, then you must try to get some sleep," Sharon urged.

"And you also," Fawn pointed out.

"I'm fine," Sharon assured her. She wouldn't be able to

sleep, anyway, she knew. "You go on to the dormitory and go to bed. The night's more than half over, as it is." She rose to her feet as she spoke.

With obvious reluctance, Fawn stood also. "I am not tired," she protested. "I can help with whatever needs to be done."

"I know." Sharon smiled with genuine warmth. "But you need some sleep, too. I'll be all right." She gripped the younger girl's hand tightly. "Thank you, Fawn."

"You'll call me if anything happens?" Fawn persisted for a moment longer.

Sharon nodded. "I promise."

"Okay." Fawn returned her smile. "I'll try to sleep until morning comes."

She started to turn away, then they both stiffened as the sound of a shot rolled through the corridors of the mission.

The echoes were confusing, but Isaac was sure the gunshot had come from the second floor of the building. He had his old Dragon Colt in his fist as he moved at a run down the hallway.

Had the enemy somehow gained access? he wondered fearfully. He saw Sharon and Fawn near one of the hall benches. The young women started to follow him as he passed, but he waved them back. He didn't turn around to see if they obeyed.

He paused at the door to the infirmary. Only moments had passed since the weapon had discharged. It had been a handgun, he was sure. No further shots had followed.

He crouched as he entered the room. The shirtless figure standing in the sickroom swiveled toward him, then swayed and almost fell. A six-gun was held awkwardly in his left hand.

Isaac let himself relax slowly. "You shouldn't be up, Marshal," he drawled. "Much less practicing with your gun."

"For pete's sake, it was just an accident! A mistake! All

right?" Stever was still swaying on his feet as he spoke. "And don't let that little nurse back in here!"

Isaac shrugged and turned to the door. Sharon and Fawn were standing behind him at a distance. He relayed Stever's explanation and closed the outer door firmly on their further questions. Then he turned his attention back to Stever.

The marshal, Isaac saw, had his injured right arm in a crude sling that he had obviously rigged himself. He had donned his gunbelt backward, so the butt of his Colt was ready for a clumsy reverse draw with his sound left hand.

Isaac slid the Dragoon back into its sheath. "You ain't too good left-handed," he commented.

"I'm fine left-handed!" Stever snapped. "I dropped the blasted thing trying to draw it, is all!"

"Uh huh." Isaac moved closer.

Stever scowled darkly, examined his Colt, then jammed it into the reversed holster. He flexed his left hand over it. Isaac marveled that the marshal was on his feet at all. Willpower and determination alone were keeping him standing there.

"Well?" Stever demanded, glaring at him.

Isaac shrugged once more. "Don't mind me. Go right ahead with what you were doing."

"That little nurse wouldn't even let me out of bed," Stever complained instead. "I had to fix this sling myself." He winced as he moved his right arm. He shook his head angrily and went on, "Then I like to never got my gunbelt on. Now I can't even draw the consarned thing without dropping it and darn near shooting myself in the foot! And don't tell me that I need to be in bed!"

Isaac studied him. "Try sticking it in your belt for a cross draw," he suggested knowledgeably.

Stever stared at him for a moment. Then he pulled the Colt and slid it under the gunbelt, butt angled to his left. He drew it, then replaced it and drew it again.

"Makes sense," he muttered.

"You still ain't no good with your left."

"I don't have much choice," Stever growled. He repeated the awkward crossdraw, and mumbled something unintelligible under his breath. "No way I can use a long gun," he concluded aloud.

Isaac let his glance rove about the room. "That your sawed-off?" he asked.

Stever grunted and came into the outer room. He looked at the corner Isaac indicated.

"Yeah, it's mine," he admitted. "But I can't use it one-handed, either." He shook his head ruefully. "Never been stove up like this before when there was work to be done. It rides a man hard."

Isaac crossed the room and picked up the shotgun. He hefted it a moment in contemplation, then offered it to Stever.

"Here. Try sticking it in your sling."

"Huh?" Stever hesitated then shoved the Colt back under his belt to accept the shotgun. He fumbled clumsily with it.

"Just a minute." Isaac took the shotgun from his hand, broke it, and checked the barrels. They were empty. He returned it to the lawman. "Don't want that one going off by accident in here," he murmured dryly.

Stever juggled the stubby weapon a moment before he managed to insert it in his sling. He used his right arm to cradle it and clamp its butt against his side. He reached across his body with his left hand and curled his fingers experimentally over the twin triggers.

"Expect you'll have to turn some sideways to use it," Isaac offered. "But you'll make a smaller target that way. Course, the recoil won't do your wounded arm no good."

"The devil with that." Stever practiced pivoting into position to fire the Greener in various directions. At last he relaxed and looked at Isaac. "Not bad," he admitted grudgingly.

"Now that you're armed to the teeth, why don't you go back to bed," Isaac suggested.

Stever didn't argue. He seemed almost grateful to comply. His legs were shaking visibly as he returned to the sickroom. He leaned the shotgun against the wall within easy reach and sat down on the bed with a relieved sigh.

Isaac stood in the doorway and regarded him. "You figure to need all that firepower?" he questioned. "I told you, Tom done hauled Tayback off to Konowa earlier this evening."

"Shoot!" Stever said through clenched teeth. "You don't think all this is really over, do you? Langston might be as good as you say, but he ain't good enough to get Tayback past his men and over those hills to Konowa single-handed. Nobody is! Langston's most likely dead by now, and Tayback and his boys are on their way back here. This mission's like a fat hen in a coop. No hungry coyote could pass it up, and Tayback's got a mighty big hunger. He'll move on us just to get me, if nothing else."

"Supposing Tom made it?"

Stever gave a cautious shrug, which didn't seem to hurt his arm too badly. "Won't make much difference. Segundo will never believe Tayback's gone until he's torn this place apart himself. Either way, you can bet trouble's coming down the pike." He fixed Isaac with a level stare from his flint eyes. "You roust me just as soon as it starts, you hear? With Langston gone, we're short a gunhand. You can't afford to be choosy. You'll need everybody you've got who can handle a gun, including a cripple like me. Understand?"

"Yessir," Isaac said. His inflection made Stever's eyes grow even harder. "Any other orders?"

Stever seemed on the verge of retorting, but he relaxed and shook his head tiredly. "Just call me, all right?" This time he made it a request.

"I reckon I'll have a use for you, if it comes to trouble," Isaac acknowledged. He turned and hobbled out of the infirmary.

They were still behind him, Tom knew. Somewhere back up in the wooded hills, Tayback and his human wolves were on the prowl. Tom hadn't heard them for some time, but he knew instinctively that they were back there.

The memory of Tayback's shouted threats hung over him like hideous, evil curses. Either following his trail, or simply moving in the same direction, he was sure Tayback was leading his men toward the mission.

Tom came riding down out of the hills. Through the woods ahead of him, the gabled shape of the mission loomed against the dim night sky like some ancient castle. Morning wasn't more than a couple of hours away. Tayback would probably arrive soon, but he might wait until daylight to act.

Tom was shivering from cold and maybe from dread, he admitted to himself. His presence at the mission might make little difference against the odds they faced. Tayback's fury would be unquenchable save by violence and death. Even with the losses in the early skirmishes with the mission he still had plenty of men backing him, including Segundo.

Briefly Tom had considered riding on to Konowa for help, once he had succeeded in evading Tayback and his band. But even if he had managed to obtain assistance and return, he figured he would've been too late to avert Tayback's onslaught on the mission.

Tiredly, he guided Paint past the other outbuildings to the stable. The mustang was plodding from exhaustion. In the stable Tom stripped off the saddle. Behind him the door creaked. He turned sharply, then relaxed as he recognized the grizzled figure there.

"You didn't make it, huh?" Isaac said.

Tom shook his head. "Tayback's loose," he reported. "He's coming this way with his pack."

Isaac moved to help him store his gear. He pulled the Winchester from its saddle sheath and handed it over. Wordlessly Tom accepted it.

"That's about the way Stever reckoned it would be," Isaac commented. "Except he figured you'd be dead."

"I almost was," Tom told him. They all might be before the day was out, he added grimly to himself.

CHAPTER 13

"SO, he's leading his men back here," Sister Mary Agnes said after hearing what had happened.

"Yes, ma'am," Tom confirmed.

Even in the poor light of her office, he could read the lines of fatigue in her austere features. The night had not been an easy one for her either, he figured. Beside him, Isaac remained silent.

"It was a very courageous and selfless thing you tried to do, Mr. Langston," she stated almost formally. "I appreciate you taking such risks on behalf of my flock. I am also glad you are alive. I feared for your safety while you were gone."

"Thank you, ma'am."

Mary Agnes lowered her face into her hands. She remained motionless like that for a long moment. At last she lifted her head. The lines of fatigue were still present, but her jaw was set in determination.

"We shall have to fight, then," she said firmly. "I do not think Mr. Tayback will offer quarter. We must be prepared to defend ourselves to the fullest extent possible."

Tom didn't comment. She had read the situation like a skilled woodsman reading a game trail.

"I had hoped it would not come to this." Resolutely she rose from her desk. "Please accompany me, gentlemen."

Without speaking further, she led them from her office and up the stairway to the third floor. In her study, she moved briskly to a large wardrobe that filled one corner of the room. She produced a key from somewhere on her person and unlocked the piece, pulling double doors wide. Tom saw some outdated clothing hanging neatly in one side of the wardrobe. Shelves on the other side contained small unmarked boxes covered with dust.

Mary Agnes bent and tugged at an object set far back in the bottom of the wardrobe. "A hand, if you will," she requested.

Tom and Isaac moved forward. She stepped aside to give them room. They drew forth a low heavy chest sealed by a padlocked hasp.

"Over here, gentlemen." She gestured to indicate a clear area of the floor.

When the chest was at her feet she knelt and used a second key on the padlock. "In addition to the girls school, there was once a school for boys here," she explained in a matter-of-fact manner, without looking up. "Almost everything was lost when that school burned. Only a few items were saved. Being of a naturally frugal nature, and thinking, perhaps, that there might someday be need of them in this relatively lawless area, I retained certain things myself. I confess I have never had occasion to examine them since I placed them here. I trust we will find them still functional."

She lifted the lid of the trunk and pulled back a layer of oilskin. Tom heard Isaac's soft whistle of surprise. The old man reached down past her and withdrew one of the old Winchester .44-.40 rifles.

"I believe they used them in a riflery course," Mary Agnes commented further. She straightened and stepped away from the chest.

Tom hunkered down and took one of the rifles himself. It looked to be in good condition. The sturdy construction of the chest and the layers of oilskin had served to protect the firearms.

There were five of the rifles in all. Tom set them carefully out, one at a time. The bottom of the chest was filled with neatly packed boxes of .44-.40 ammunition. Tom opened one of the boxes. He extracted a cartridge and examined it, then passed it to Isaac. The old man knelt beside him and turned it over and over in his fingers. He grunted approval.

"Well, gentlemen?" Mary Agnes prompted.

Isaac tilted his head up. "You never told me you had a regular arsenal here, Sister," he said in wonder.

"There was never any need," she answered gently. The lines in her face deepened. "I do not approve of guns or killing. But I will not stand foolishly by and see innocents slaughtered by pagans such as Mr. Tayback and his followers. I don't understand my calling to prohibit self-defense under such circumstances. At the trial of our Lord, when a Roman soldier attempted to strike him, he rebuked the soldier for doing so. I think, gentlemen, it is time we rebuked Mr. Tayback, as well."

"Amen, Sister," Isaac whispered fervently.

Her face severe, she bent, picked up one of the rifles, and levered it competently to be sure it was unloaded. Her hands were quite steady, Tom noted with admiration.

"I will use one myself," she declared. "It is a poor shepherd who will not stand to defend the flock. Sister Lenora and Sister Ruth can also be armed. Miss Easton and Fawn have both indicated their willingness to assist in the active defense of the school. I rejected their offers when they spoke of it to me. Now I believe it is time to call upon them." She calculated briefly, then continued, "I assume it would be wise for each of you to retain your handguns in addition to utilizing your own rifles."

"I think so, ma'am," Isaac said as crisply as if he were responding to a senior officer.

"What about Marshal Stever?" Mary Agnes inquired.

Isaac straightened to his feet and stood almost at attention. "He says he can fight, Sister. I ain't so sure—leastways, he won't be using his rifle. I reckon he'll hang onto that sawed-off and his six-gun, unless we take them away by force."

"Then his rifle makes one extra gun," Mary Agnes concluded. "I shall request a capable volunteer from among the students. That will make nine armed defenders. Where do you suggest we station ourselves to prepare for combat?"

Isaac glanced briefly at Tom, then figured aloud. "I guess three on each of the first two floors, two on the third, and one in the cupola ought to do it. Me and Tom and the marshal, if he can manage it, should be on the ground floor in case things get close. Sister, you and the students will need to cover the top two floors. We'll help you pick the windows that give the widest fields of fire. Your best marksman should be in the cupola." He glanced once more at Tom in silent acknowledgment. "We'll need to cover both the front and back."

Mary Agnes nodded as he spoke. "Very well." She looked back and forth between them. "And what other preparations do we need to make?"

Isaac jerked his head at Tom. "He called it once before, when I asked him."

"The first-floor windows should be boarded up or barricaded, leaving some kind of rifle port in as many as possible," Tom told her. He recalled his earlier discussion with Isaac. "The firing sites on the other floors will need some sort of protection as well—mattresses, furniture, things that can slow or stop a bullet. We'll also need a couple of runners who can keep Isaac and me informed if someone upstairs spots something outside that we can't see from down on the first floor."

He drew a deep breath, still speaking thoughts aloud. "All the rest of the students should be confined to inside rooms on the upper floors. If they are in rooms with windows, then they need to stay on the floor." He fell silent and regarded Mary Agnes steadily. "We ain't talking about no Sunday church social here, Sister. When those boys come, they'll come shooting. It'll be dangerous for anybody shooting back."

The gaze of the headmistress was as steady as his own. "Won't the ultimate danger be even greater if we do not take steps to defend ourselves?" she asked flatly.

There was iron in her, Tom mused. If anything, the events of the past day and night had only served to harden the metal.

"We better get to work," he said.

"I shall call an assembly immediately," Mary Agnes declared. She left them there in her study.

Within the hour Tom found himself with the Sister, facing the assemblage of students and teachers seated at tables in the dining hall. Isaac had avoided the gathering to stand watch.

Tom saw Sharon's face among the ranks of his audience. Her hair shone like dark spun gold in the dim light of the big room. She had an expression of mingled relief and apprehension. Tom regretted that there had not been an opportunity for more than a brief formal greeting in the company of Mary Agnes upon his return.

Stever was not present. Tom had stopped by the infirmary while Mary Agnes gathered the students. The lawman had stared darkly at him for a moment.

"Didn't expect to see you again, Langston," Stever said. "What happened?"

Briefly, Tom told him.

The lawman shook his head as Tom finished. "I could've told you there was no way in thunder it would work," he admonished.

"I expect you could've," Tom drawled.

"What were you thinking of to try a tinhorn stunt like that, anyway?" Stever pressed relentlessly.

"Right now, I'm thinking I should've left you back in that cabin to freeze some of the orneriness out of you."

Stever's mouth tightened. "Nobody asked you to haul me and my prisoner here!"

"Nobody asked me to save your life, either!" Tom snapped. He pivoted on his heel toward the door.

"Langston!" Stever's voice stopped him before he made it out of the room.

He turned reluctantly back. "Yeah?" he asked harshly.

Stever motioned vaguely with his good hand. "You did your best," he admitted grudgingly. "I reckon it was as good as I could've done."

That was about the limit of any apology he was going to get, Tom decided. "Looks like it wasn't enough, though," he conceded.

"So what are you and the old man doing to get ready?" An undertone of skepticism still rode Stever's words.

Tom related their plans. When he finished the lawman shook his head and said, "A bunch of nuns and schoolgirls to take on the toughest pack of owlhoots in the Territory."

"And one stove-up marshal," Tom added curtly. "Any suggestions for improvement?"

"Sounds like you and the old man have it covered. I'll back you when the time comes."

"Sure." Tom left him to his brooding.

As Tom faced the nuns and the students, the lawman's words and attitude still rankled him, but he tried to put the feelings aside. Stever was a wounded pro forced to rely on what he considered amateurs to do his job while he stood helplessly by.

Sister Mary Agnes completed her terse explanations, and led a short prayer. Afterward she announced, "Mr. Langston will address you now. Pay close attention to what he says."

Tom stared at the dark-haired feminine faces watching him intently. The students ranged from ten to seventeen years old. He saw expressions of concern, excitement, and simply no emotion at all. He spotted Fawn sitting next to Sharon with the nuns at a table on the edge of the gathering. The bright look of encouragement in Sharon's blue eyes was strengthening.

"You heard what the Sister said," he began awkwardly. "There ain't no hiding the danger we're in, but we're not giving up without showing them a fight." He went on to describe the defensive arrangements in general terms. "Rifles will be issued to all faculty members," he added. "In addition, we'll need two students who can use rifles."

Immediately Fawn raised her hand. Several other girls followed suit a moment later.

"All right, Fawn," Tom told the tall girl. She smiled tightly and turned to whisper to Sharon. Tom glanced to Mary Agnes for help.

"Songbird," Mary Agnes addressed one of the other girls whose hand was uplifted.

"Yes, ma'am," the girl responded in a melodious voice as she rose to her feet.

"Can you use a rifle?" the headmistress questioned.

Unsmiling, Songbird nodded. She was shorter and heavier than Fawn. "Often I have hunted with my brothers and my father," she elaborated. "On the reservation we had little to eat, and it was necessary for all of us to hunt in order to live."

"Very well." Mary Agnes accepted her. "Thank you for volunteering." She glanced at Tom with a slight nod of approval. The other raised hands among the girls were lowered.

"The rest of you will need to help barricade the windows," Tom told them. "Time is short. Sister, can you distribute the rifles and the ammunition?"

Mary Agnes nodded.

Tom divided the remaining girls into work crews. The largest group of ten girls he assigned to the ground floor. He placed the other two crews under the supervision of Sister Ruth and Sister Lenora. He and Mary Agnes served as overseers for all three crews.

The cellar yielded some old mattresses, as well as odds and ends of ancient lumber, packing crates, and damaged furniture. These provided the raw materials for the defenses. The students set willingly to the labor. Soon the halls echoed with the sounds of hammering and sawing, intermingled with the chatter of high-pitched voices.

Tom prowled the floors, overseeing the work and picking sites for the defenders to occupy. As the nuns and selected students reported for duty with the rifles distributed by Mary Agnes, he checked the firearms. All of the old guns seemed to be in good shape. He did not want to risk test-firing them for fear of revealing the capabilities of the defenders to Tayback, should the outlaw be within earshot. Tom doubted Tayback would be expecting much in the way of defense from the mission. Tom hoped he would be in for a grim surprise.

"Don't shoot wild or blind," he told the riflers when he had them all together for a last time in the dining hall. "Our ammo's limited, and we can't afford to waste it. Wait until your shots count something. That don't mean you have to have a sure hit before you cut loose. Scaring a man can sometimes be almost as effective as shooting him. And these guys will be shooting back, so be careful. I don't guess I need to tell you to stay under cover as much as possible." He paused. "Any questions?"

They stared back at him with expressions ranging from the stern resolve of Sister Mary Agnes to the obvious apprehension of Sister Ruth. Three nuns, two Indian girls, and a young schoolteacher to man the guns of the mission, he mused ruefully. He offered up a silent prayer himself.

"We will fight, Mr. Langston," Sister Mary Agnes assured him. She might almost have read his thoughts.

"I know, ma'am," he said.

He didn't doubt their willingness. But would their efforts be enough against the likes of Tayback and his crew?

"Report to your stations," he ordered crisply.

As they dispersed, he drew Sharon aside. "You watch out," he told her quietly.

She nodded and gave him a timorous smile. "You also." For a moment she hesitated, as if there was more she wanted to say. He thought of the things he himself had left unspoken

between them. There was no time now. He might already
have waited too late.

She turned suddenly from him and hurried away. He
watched her go with a pang in his heart.

Isaac appeared from the hallway. He noted Tom's gaze
following the departing girl. "How are the troops?" he asked
after a moment.

Tom shrugged. "They'll fight."

Isaac grunted in wordless comment. "Never seen the Sister
quite like that before," he said then. "I've seen her face up to
lots of things, from the pestilence to angry Indians. She's
brave, sure enough. But she's always been a peaceable
woman."

"She still is," Tom said. He thought of a mother puma
defending her cubs against the hunters.

"I expect so," Isaac acknowledged after a moment. He
hefted his carbine. "Almost daylight outside. I seen movement up in the hills. I figure they're up there, watching and
waiting."

"They'll be coming soon," Tom said with certainty.

"We could be in real trouble if they make a siege out of it.
Our supplies won't last forever."

"We're already in real trouble. But Tayback won't make it a
siege. He can't be sure how long the bad weather will hold
out. Somebody will be coming up from Konowa to check on
things eventually. Besides, Tayback ain't in the mood to sit
back and starve us out. He'll want it over fast and hard. He's
hungry for killing."

"Well, I guess we're as ready for him as we can get." Isaac's
brow furrowed thoughtfully. "I reckon I know a little now
how those Johnny Rebs felt in Fort Wagner, waiting for us
Yankees to march on them."

"Where's Stever?" Tom asked.

"He's covering the back. He don't like it because he don't
have a clear field of fire from them high windows. But he
agreed as to how somebody needed to be back there, and

that he was the best choice. He still ain't moving none too good, and his right arm ain't worth nothing." Isaac considered for a moment. "Come to close fighting, he might do all right," he allowed at last.

Tom pulled his Colt and checked the loads. He replaced the gun in its holster. Then he picked up his Winchester from where he had leaned it against the wall.

"Let's go wait for them," he said.

CHAPTER 14

THE gunfire began with daylight. From a half-dozen points up in the hills, rifles spoke and bullets thudded into the walls of the mission or broke glass to embed themselves in the boards and mattresses of the barricades.

From where he crouched beside a ground-floor window, Tom squinted up at the wooded slopes. The sharpshooters were well concealed, and the white snow cast a glare even under the clouded sky. Only an occasional wisp of smoke drifted up to betray the location of a rifleman.

A bullet ricocheted off the outer wall mere inches from the window where he knelt. Tom spotted a trace of smoke from under a distant evergreen. He brought his Winchester to his shoulder, sighted carefully, and fired. He couldn't tell if he had hit anything or not. Had he seen the smoke at all? he asked himself.

Another bullet struck the wall immediately above the window. Tom hunkered low behind his barrier of dismantled packing crates. He scowled darkly. Tayback was being more cunning than he had expected. The outlaw was using rifle fire to unnerve the defenders before he made a frontal attack.

Tom wondered how things were upstairs, how well they were holding up under the prolonged sharpshooting. By his own orders the women were not to return fire at this stage. He didn't want to give away the presence of so many armed defenders. Besides, he doubted whether any of the women had the experience to hit such distant targets.

A bullet thudded solidly against the boards covering the window next to his position. Tom heard a wordless snarl of frustration from Isaac, further down the hall. The old man left his position and scuttled along the corridor to crouch beside Tom.

"I done had enough of this tomfoolery!" he snapped. "Can't hit nothing in those hills from down here. I'm going up top in the cupola and give them varmints something to chew on!"

"Keep your head down," Tom advised.

Isaac grinned. "Teach your grandpappy how to plow, son!" he retorted. He took off in the direction of the stairway.

Tom frowned and sent another shot at the distant evergreen. He was probably just wasting ammo, he told himself sourly.

The gunfire certainly was serving to soften them up, but it might have another purpose as well, he reasoned. He didn't think there were more than six riflemen firing on the mission. Where were the rest of the outlaws? Tom studied the outbuildings. They would make for good cover, but he saw nothing in their vicinity to alarm him. Just the same, they bore watching.

From far above came the muffled report of Isaac's carbine. Tom grinned. He remembered Isaac's accuracy with the old rifle during the skirmish the night before. He moved to another window and loosed off a shot himself. Give them something to chew on, he thought.

Isaac reloaded and adjusted the frayed brim of his cavalry hat. It made no difference. The dull glare from the snow still distorted his vision. Just have to put up with it, he decided.

He propped the barrel of the carbine on the window ledge of the cupola and waited patiently. You didn't get to be an old black man without learning something about patience, he mused wryly.

His reward came in the form of a bullet whining off the cupola just above his small window vantage point. He ducked involuntarily, but he was sure he had seen the glint of metal and a wisp of smoke from a thicket cloaking the lower trunks of a grove of saplings.

Whoever the owlhoot sharpshooter was, he had spotted him in the cupola very soon after his first shot from that position. The fellow had keen eyes and was a good shot. Isaac wondered suddenly if he was again trading bullets with the same hombre he had dueled with while in the cupola the night before. He was somehow sure that he was.

He allowed himself a grin, and sighted down the barrel of the carbine. The old cavalry gun wasn't meant for long-range shooting. But he had carried it with him for so long, and used it so many times over the years when his life hung in the balance, that he thought of it as almost a part of himself. When a shot was good it was as easy and natural as pointing his finger. Just like knowing where he pointed, he knew when a bullet went true.

He took his time, calculating the wind, the glare from the snow, and the distance. Another bullet chipped fragments from the cupola. This time he didn't flinch at all. He rolled his head around on his neck, settled the carbine more firmly against his shoulder, and sighted carefully on the distant thicket. When everything felt right, he squeezed the trigger.

Like pointing his finger. He had an impression of a flurry of movement in the thicket. Then it was still. Satisfied, he drew the carbine back to reload. That particular owlhoot would be doing no more sharpshooting, he was certain.

The firing had slackened, he noted. There seemed fewer riflemen targeting the mission now, even allowing for his hit. He frowned against the cold air on his face. What had happened to the other sharpshooters? He focused his eyes lower down on the hillsides. After an interval he began to detect movement. It was no more than vague impressions of mounted figures descending through the brush and woodland. They were too indefinite for targets.

He switched his attention to the outbuildings. It was almost a minute before he caught a flicker of movement from the far corner of the barn. If he had not been up high, he would've missed it.

Grimly he drew back from the window. The softening-up process was finished. Tayback and his men were coming out of the hills to attack.

Isaac dropped agilely down the ladder from the trapdoor. The Indian girl, Songbird, was awaiting him. She had been occupying the cupola before he had ousted her. As she saw the expression on his face, her dark eyes grew wide with anxiety.

"Go on back up," he told her. "But you be careful, girl. Keep your head down as much as you can. They're moving up behind the outbuildings. Watch real sharp."

She nodded and scrambled up the ladder. Isaac sought out Sharon and Fawn where they crouched at two of the windows. They both looked around at the sound of his approach. He wasted no time in repeating his message and warning. Both young women nodded. They looked apprehensive, he thought. But he read determination in their faces as well.

He descended to the second floor. Mary Agnes listened silently as he spoke.

"We shall be ready, Isaac," she stated when he was finished.

"Yes, ma'am."

"I believe you hit one of them at a considerable distance with your last shot," she noted aloud.

He stared at her in wonder. "I believe I did too, ma'am."

"It was an exceptional shot."

He thought he managed to keep the pleasure he felt at her praise from showing on his face. "Thank you, Sister."

Her crisp nod dismissed him.

"They're behind the buildings," Isaac reported tersely.

"I seen them," Tom told him. "I ain't been able to get a shot yet, though."

He eyed the old man. Isaac looked fit and vigorous. His movements were lively, almost youthful.

"You got lucky with that one," Tom said, referring to Isaac's earlier shot.

"Luck, my foot, boy!" Isaac snapped with a pleased grin. "But don't you fret none. You'll be having some easy targets, more to your liking, before too long, unless I miss my guess." He moved on past Tom and chose another window a distance down the hall.

"Any activity out back?" Tom called to him.

Isaac shook his head. "Stever's doing fine back there. I stopped by and told him they was coming."

Tom nodded and looked once more toward the barn and other structures. A few desultory shots still rang out from the hills. He guessed Tayback and most of his men were bunched now behind the outbuildings. A bitter frustration at his helplessness rode him cruelly.

"You tell the women?" he thought to ask Isaac.

"I told them. They're ready."

Tom spotted a mounted figure near the stable. He jerked his rifle up, but the figure was gone before he could draw a bead. He felt a pang of worry for Paint and the other mounts if the gunfire got heavy.

A fusillade of shots erupted. Six-guns and rifles blasted from at least four different points about the structures. Tom could only duck behind his makeshift barrier as the bullets slammed into the wood or ricocheted from the walls. The outlaws had targeted the ground-floor windows, he realized. Could be they had detected his and Isaac's presence.

The shooting tapered abruptly, then stopped. An order had been given. Tom lifted his head and swept the Winchester to his shoulder. He was none too soon. Horsemen erupted from behind the cover of the structures, six-guns blazing.

The outlaws were charging the mission, hoping to reach it along the shoveled paths or over the hardened snow. Tom

held his fire. Once they were fully in the open they would
make easy targets for the waiting defenders inside.

From above Tom heard the muffled crack of a single rifle.
It was too soon, he thought dismally. The attackers weren't
yet clear of the cover of the outbuildings. He saw one burly
rider pull his roan rearing up. He recognized Tayback. In
the same moment a ragged volley of shots sounded from
overhead, kicking up snow and splintering the walls of the
buildings. Sparked by the early shot, the remaining defenders had opened fire before they had clear targets.

Tom ground his teeth together in frustration and shifted
his Winchester to bear on one of the enemy. He actually
heard Tayback's voice bawling commands. The riders, meeting the unexpected resistance, were swinging their horses
about to regain the cover of the buildings. Tom loosed off a
shot. He saw the rider reel in the saddle as his horse disappeared from sight behind Isaac's cabin. A hit, he thought
darkly, but probably not a clean one. His target might well
be able to carry on the fight.

He swept his rifle in an arc to find Tayback, but the outlaw
chieftan had disappeared with his men. Incredibly, not a one
of them had gone down.

Tom slumped with a sigh of regret. In a matter of moments they had given up their advantage of surprise, and
they had nothing to show for it but a single wounded enemy.

"You got one, leastways," Isaac's weighted voice reached
him.

"Just nicked him, I think."

"Better than me." Isaac sounded old now. "Didn't even get
off a shot. Not one."

"Who you reckon it was loosed off that first round?" Tom
asked. He thought he knew the answer.

Isaac pondered a moment. "My guess would be Sister
Ruth. She's sweet, but she weren't cut out for no gunfights."

Remembering the naked apprehension he had seen earlier
in the soft face of the nun, Tom figured Isaac was right.

Mary Agnes had provided him with a small handbell to summon the two girls who were to serve as runners. He used it now. One of the girls appeared shortly.

"Check and make sure there haven't been casualties," Tom told her. He thought for a brief interval. "Tell them I said we did good to repulse the attack, but they need to watch their shots and not waste ammo."

The girl nodded and hurried off.

"You fixing to run for office?" Isaac jibed. "That was a politician talking if I ever heard one!"

"You were in the cavalry," Tom reminded him. "You ought to know about keeping up the morale of the troops."

Tom figured Tayback would now know that he faced not a pair of gunmen, but a substantial force of armed defenders. He would be wary of any more direct frontal assaults. The presence of the defenders would make him more careful in how he risked his men.

"*Cowdog?*" Tom stiffened as Tayback's voice came rolling across the space between the mission and the other structures. "You in there?"

Tom felt Isaac's eyes on him from down the corridor. "I'm here!" he shouted out the window into the cold.

"What do you think you're doing, giving rifles to all them nuns?" Tayback's sardonic disembodied voice came back.

"Come on and find out!" Tom shouted the challenge.

"We aim to do that, cowdog, and when we do, you're just going to get all them nuns and squaws hurt trying to fight us off!"

"The way I read it, they'll get hurt anyway!" Tom hollered back. The cold air burned his throat.

Tayback's brazen laughter echoed. "You done got that right, cowdog. Why not just open them doors and make things easy on me and my boys?"

"Why not come out with your hands up?" Tom shot back. "You and all your men!" He wondered vaguely what Sister Mary Agnes was making of this schoolboy exchange.

"No thanks, cowdog. I've had enough of being your prisoner. I ain't going to let it happen again. I might not be able to get away a second time." There was a pause, as if Tayback was drawing breath to continue. "How many guns you got in there, anyway?"

"I told you, come and find out!"

"Is that filthy old slave the sharpshooter who got one of my boys way back up there in the brush?"

"You willing to face off with six-guns with that 'filthy old-slave'?" Tom challenged.

"Not today, cowdog, but I'm going to enjoy killing him almost as much as I'll enjoy killing you."

"You ain't done too well, so far."

"What about the marshal? Is he dead yet?"

"I'm here, Tayback!" the familiar voice shouted unexpectedly past Tom's ear.

Tom turned and saw the spectral figure of Stever close beside him. The marshal's approach had been eerily silent. His Colt was jammed in his gunbelt, the butt angled toward his left hand. His shotgun was carried in his sling. The planes of his bearded face were drawn sharp with pain. The effort of shouting had clearly hurt him. Tom drew back to let him come nearer. Stever propped himself against the wall beside the window.

"I thought plumb sure you'd be dead by now, lawdog!" Tayback called.

"Not hardly!"

"Well, I'll see if I can't fix that real soon!" Tayback's evil laughter boomed again.

"Turn yourself in, Tayback," Stever tried. "At least, leave these womenfolk alone!"

"Too late for that, lawdog! Now I got a personal score to settle with that holier-than-thou nun, as well as you and the cowdog!"

Anger swept away the pain on Stever's features. Left-handed he pulled his Colt. "Settle this, Tayback!" he shouted, and fired out the window in the direction of the outbuildings.

The shot rang into silence. Momentarily Tom expected the outlaws to start firing. But there was no response to the words or the gun. Tayback's voice did not sound again.

Stever drew away from the window. Awkwardly he jammed the gun into his belt. He stood erect with an effort.

"I'll cover the back," he growled, and hobbled away.

"I better go check how they're handling all this upstairs," Tom told Isaac.

The older man glanced around from his window. "You're awful free and easy challenging owlhoots to gunfights on my behalf!" he complained.

Tom grinned at him. "I wasn't worried," he explained. "I was going to back you up so you didn't get hurt none." He turned away on Isaac's exasperated snort.

Mary Agnes met him as he topped the stairs on the second floor. "I apologize, Mr. Langston," she spoke without preamble. "It will not happen again, I assure you."

"Sister Ruth?" Tom inquired quietly.

She nodded confirmation. "I should've anticipated it, knowing her nature as I do. She became frightened and fired too soon."

Tom hitched his shoulders in an uncomfortable shrug. "Can't be helped now," he said gruffly. "And don't be too hard on her. I've seen greenhorns and veteran lawmen alike lose their nerve under a charge like that."

Mary Agnes nodded stiffly. "Thank you. I shall tell her that. I have already spoken to her. She is very contrite and is determined to do well in the future. I'm sure she shall."

Tom hoped bleakly that they had enough of a future to give her a chance. "Everything else all right?" he queried aloud. "No casualties?"

"None, Mr. Langston. But in that regard, I have arranged for another capable student to stand by to replace Sister Lenora should her nursing skills be required."

"Good idea, Sister," Tom praised. It was something he should've thought of, he reflected.

He left the headmistress with her subordinates and mounted to the third floor, where Sharon and Fawn kept watch. Sharon saw him. Carefully she set her rifle aside, rose from where she crouched at a window, and came toward him.

Tom felt the sudden grip of relief at seeing her unharmed. He was surprised at the strength of the emotion.

She slowed her pace as she drew near to him. "Is—everything all right?" she asked hesitantly.

Tom found suddenly that he couldn't speak. Without planning it, he reached out and hugged her to him. He felt her arms lift eagerly to cling to him. Vaguely he was aware of Fawn watching them from a barricaded window further down the room. She turned her head away; he thought she had been smiling.

He tightened his hold briefly, then reluctantly loosened it. Sharon stepped back with what seemed equal reluctance. Her face was uplifted so she could see his features.

"Oh, Tom," she breathed. "I prayed nothing would happen to you." She hesitated, and almost stammered as she added in a whisper, "To us."

"Yeah," Tom said hoarsely. Some hardened part of his mind told him he needed to return below as soon as possible. He forced his attention off the brightness in her face and eyes. "It's not over yet," he told her bluntly. "They're still out there."

She bowed her head briefly. "I know." He barely caught her voice. "We could hear you and that awful Tayback shouting back and forth." She lifted her head. "After the shooting started, Fawn and I both fired, but I don't think we hit anything."

Beyond her, Tom saw Fawn suddenly flinch away from her position with a startled cry. He had only a fleeting sight of the burning missile that streaked through the window and buried itself in the folded mattresses that had served as her barricade. With horror, he recognized it as a fire arrow. Almost instantly yellow flames leapt upward from the piled bedding.

CHAPTER 15

TOM snatched the shaft of the arrow and plucked it free. The tip had been wrapped in rags drenched with coal oil before being set afire. It still burned fiercely, the flames seeming to lick at his face and arm. He hurled it out from the window, not bothering to see where it fell. He grabbed the mattress and flipped it over to smother the flames against the flagstones of the floor. Acrid smoke billowed up. He had a brief glimpse of Fawn scrambling determinedly back to the window, rifle in hand.

Sharon cried out from where he had left her in his dash to reach the arrow. Glass shattered as he wheeled toward her. Another fire arrow had crashed through an unprotected window and thudded into the wall. Reacting, Sharon sprang forward and yanked it free. She dashed it to the floor and stamped the flame out.

Fawn's rifle cracked and boomed. Tom moved swiftly to the nearest window.

"I cannot see anyone, Mr. Langston!" Fawn cried, with frustration in her voice.

Another flaming arrow came arcing in toward a lower window from somewhere among the outbuildings. A moment later one more rose high into the air from the same source. It disappeared from sight above the windows. Involuntarily Tom cocked his head to look up at the ceiling. He knew the burning missile had landed on the roof.

Furiously he flung his rifle to his shoulder and fired in the direction from which the arrow had come. He was shooting blind. He could see no sign of the archer's whereabouts.

Two more arrows flicked upward, one after the other in

rapid succession. Both disappeared overhead. Tom imagined he could hear them thudding into the roof above. They had come from a different spot in back of the buildings than the earlier arrows.

The bowman was firing from behind the outbuildings, apparently moving after each shot or two, he was dropping the arrows into and on the mission with devilish accuracy. Tom recalled the long-haired rider with a bow and arrows he had seen among Tayback's men and wondered whether he was the mysterious archer.

Tom swept his rifle barrel across the frontage of the buildings, vainly seeking a target. There was no gunfire accompanying the barrage of arrows, he realized. That was odd.

"Mr. Langston!" one of the runners gasped as she reached his side.

He pulled her swiftly clear of the window. "What is it?" he demanded tersely.

Her dark eyes were wide. "Marshal Stever says he's spotted the outlaws gathering in the woods out back. He sent me to get you. He says you must come quickly! They are preparing to rush us!"

Abruptly Tom understood that Tayback's earlier shouted conversation with him had been much more than a whim or an effort to learn something about the mission's defenders. It had also served as a ploy to distract their attention while the majority of his men circled behind the mission.

Using the flaming arrows as another diversion, he undoubtedly planned to launch an assault against the rear of the building, in spite of the high windows and single door. But Stever's sharp eyes had spotted the deployment in time.

Another arrow sailed high over the outbuildings and dropped like a meteor toward the roof. Tom could feel the dark eyes of the runner fixed on him expectantly. Once more he glanced at the ceiling, imagining the arrows falling onto the roof. The snow would serve to extinguish the flames and prevent them from igniting the shingles, for a few moments at least.

He gave a tight nod. "Alert everyone to shift positions to the back," he commanded.

Briefly he caught Sharon's reaching hand. Her fingers gripped his tightly. He carried the yearning look in her blue eyes with him as he raced down the stairs.

Isaac met him at the foot of the stairway. The old man's black face was grim. "They're fixing to rush the back."

Tom guessed his own face was probably just as grim. "I know," he said. "But you'll have to hold them off. I've got to go after that archer."

Isaac's fingers clamped on his arm and seemed to sink to the bone. "This ain't nighttime! You're the one told me once that we needed to fight from in here and let them take the outbuildings!"

"And have that bowman smoke us out like coyotes or burn the place down?" Tom retorted angrily. He wrenched his arm free.

"But you can't reach them buildings without crossing the open in broad daylight!"

"Tayback will have most or all of his men around back by now," Tom argued urgently. "Maybe you couldn't see it from down here, but that bowman's dropping those arrows smack on the roof."

"I seen it," Isaac growled. "I just don't like the idea of you going out there, is all."

"I don't like it, either."

Isaac held his gaze for a moment longer, then shook his grizzled head in frustration. "Stay in them paths I shoveled, and keep low," he advised shortly.

"Yeah. I'll go out one of the windows." Tom moved briskly past him.

"At least, I can give you some cover," Isaac offered as he fell into step beside him.

"Only if I come under fire," Tom cautioned. "Otherwise,

any gunfire from the front of the mission will only draw attention to me."

Isaac grunted assent. Tom collected his mackinaw from the coatstand near the door. The broken windows had given a chill to the corridor. The warmth of the coat was welcome. He pushed fresh cartridges into the Winchester before donning his gloves. Then he crossed to a window and moved the barricade aside.

"Stay low," Isaac said gruffly.

"I heard you the first time."

"I'm an old man. I repeat myself sometimes!" Isaac snapped.

"I'll stay low."

Tom took a last searching look from the window then swung a leg over the sill and clambered out. He figured he was doing fair when he dropped to the snow and no bullets struck him.

He glimpsed the flaming arc of yet another arrow. The archer was concentrating on getting his arrows onto the roof or into the upper windows. He wasn't paying any attention to the ground floor.

Just keep it up, fellow, Tom thought grimly. He scuttled to the nearest path and dropped into it. The snow made a two-foot wall on either side of him. He didn't waste time looking back. At a crouching run, rifle ready to fire from the waist, he dashed the length of the path toward the barn.

He fetched up hard against the barn, and stayed there, panting, the cold air searing his lungs. Where was his prey? If he waited until the archer launched another arrow, he could get some idea of the man's location from the missile's trajectory. He gripped the Winchester and kept his eyes moving, seeking the telltale meteoric streak of another of the fire arrows.

He guessed a full minute went by, then another. He felt an involuntary frown pull at the numbed muscles of his face. Something was wrong. Too much time had passed between arrows. For some reason, the archer had halted his barrage. Was it because he had seen Tom make his dash from the mission, but had not had time to react? Was he, even now, stalking him with his lethal weapon at ready?

Tom swung his head left and right. He saw no sign of his enemy. The barn was in the center of the three outbuildings. To his left was the stable and its attached lean-to. Isaac's cabin was to his right. The barn was not a good place from which to begin a stalk. His foe could be to either side of him. He needed to start at one end of the line of the buildings and work the length of the line, from one structure to the next. That way he could be sure his enemy was not behind him.

He moved to the corner of the barn, sank to one knee, and sneaked a glance around it. The lane between the barn and the stable was clear, although he glimpsed trampled snow at its far end. Doubtless that was from the feet of the outlaws and their horses who had been lurking behind these buildings. There was no other trace of them now, but an unnerving thought stabbed at Tom. What if more than one outlaw had remained behind the protection of the buildings?

Tom pondered desperately. The fact that he had not been spotted and fired on during his mad rush from the mission probably meant the bowman was by himself. Another outlaw, if present, would have been covering the front of the mission and would not have missed Tom's exit. Likely, Tayback had moved all of his other men to the rear of the mission, leaving the archer here to distract the defenders.

Tom ground his teeth together until he could hear them. There were too many questions he couldn't answer, but he had been in one position long enough. He needed to move. He checked the lane again, sucked his lungs full of the freezing air, and dodged across the passage to the shelter of the stable.

He paused again and calculated. The bowman would need a fire to ignite his arrows. The logical place for it would be in the forge of the blacksmith's shop in the barn. He had seen no smoke, but the fire would not need to be large, and the wind would quickly dissipate smoke rising from the small chimney.

Cautiously he crept to the closed doors of the stable. He knew that he would make an excellent target for anyone looking toward the building's front from the direction of the mission. It couldn't be helped.

He crouched and tried to peer between the massive hanging doors into the building's interior. He could make out the dim figures of the mules and horses in their pens and stalls. He heard their shufflings and wrinkled his nose at their pungent odor. He could detect nothing human.

He recalled from Isaac's tour that there were single doors at either end of the stable. The lean-to was at the rear. He continued to the far corner and dodged around it. More trampled snow was in evidence here. He stayed close to the building's wall as he moved to the rear corner of the lean-to. The faint crunching of his booted feet on the snow seemed loud in his ears.

He risked a glance around the corner. He could see all the way down the line of the three adjacent buildings. There was no sign of his elusive prey. A chicken cackled at his presence from within the lean-to. Others joined it. He berated them silently as he hastily retraced his steps to the side door.

He went through it fast and stepped sideways so he would not be silhouetted. The huge shadowy forms of the horses and mules shifted and snorted in the darkness. He could see nothing else.

He worked his way forward to the opposite door and let himself out. He sprang across the alleyway between the buildings and flattened his shoulders against the wall of the barn.

His heart seemed to punch at the inside of his rib cage. He remembered the speed with which the archer had been able to launch his arrows. A good bowman, holding spare arrows in the same fist that gripped the bow, could twitch a shaft up with his fingers and have it nocked in the blink of an eye. He could loose arrows almost as rapidly as a man could thumb and fire a six-gun.

Tom slipped to the corner of the barn and checked the rear of the line of buildings once again. The tall double doors in the back of the barn stood open. It was in and around the barn that the outlaws must've clustered, he guessed. Was the bowman in there now? Tom tried to remember the layout of the barn from his previous visit. Cautiously he edged to the side of the doorway.

He could hear nothing beyond the sigh of the wind playing through the old building. He used his rifle to feint an entry, snapping it out in front of the doorway as if about to duck around into the barn. There was no reaction from within. Tom had the sudden icy feeling that he was stalking a wraith. He glanced nervously over his shoulder at the woods to his back. Maybe the bowman was not even among the buildings. Maybe he was sighting down an arrow from the cover of the trees right now.

In a single swift movement Tom slid around the edge of the doorjamb and into the cavernous gloom of the barn, rifle leveled. Haylofts were high on either side of the central hallway. To his right was Isaac's blacksmith shop with its crippled wagon. His eye caught the gleam of coals in the open forge. He had been right. The bowman must've been using the forge to ignite his arrows.

Staying to the shadows, Tom took a step forward, then another. He halted again, his senses straining. From up above him in the opposite hayloft, he heard the faint unmistakable creak of a bow being pulled to full draw. He sprang backward as the bowstring twanged. The whipping air from the arrow's passage lashed at his face. The arrow struck full the glowing coals in the forge, and sparks exploded upward like a shower of fire. In that flaring light he saw the bowman poised in the hayloft, another arrow already flicking into place from those gripped in his fist. There was no time to aim the Winchester. Tom swiveled and fired upward, levered and fired again. The spears of flame stabbed blindingly from the rifle's barrel; the sound of the shots boomed within the confines of the barn. The shadowy figure of the bowman lurched forward and plunged headlong from the loft.

Tom sidestepped and sank to one knee. He waited, his head turning as his eyes probed the darkness. Nothing else moved in the barn. The echoes of the shots chased each other into silence. The glow of the scattered coals gradually dimmed.

Tom rose and catfooted to the fallen figure. The bow and several arrows were scattered near one outstretched hand. Tom pressed his boot down on the frozen clawing fingers, but gained no response. The bowman was dead.

He used his boot to flip the body over on its back. The pale face of the long-haired outlaw stared up dully at him in the dim light.

The man must have seen him approach from the mission, Tom reasoned. Rather than stalking him, the bowman had simply climbed to the hayloft and waited like a skilled deer hunter waiting in a tree for his target. Unlike deer, Tom had been able to shoot back.

Tom left him there and went to the front doors of the barn. They were closed, but there was enough space between them to see outside. For the first time since he exited through the window, he looked back toward the mission. Instantly he sucked in his breath. Flames danced wickedly on one end of the long roof. The bowman's arrows had done their job. Tom heaved the doors open. He heard gunfire erupt from behind the mission. He began to run. With the building aflame, Tayback and his men were launching their attack.

Isaac could smell smoke. He hoped it was his imagination, but guessed fearfully that it was not. He thought of the Sister and the other women on the upper floors of the building.

He could not go to them. If he did, Stever would be left alone to defend the rear of the mission from the coming attack.

And it would come any minute now, he was certain. Through the long head-high windows in the dining hall where he and the marshal waited, he could catch glimpses of the outlaws lurking in the woods.

"You could try to pick a few of them off with that antique of yours," Stever growled from the far end of the dining hall. He held his revolver awkwardly in his left hand. The sawed-off shotgun rode in the sling, cradled by his injured arm.

"I reckon I'll let them go ahead and rush us," Isaac answered his suggestion. "That way, I'll have a clear shot."

"By then, it might be too late."

Isaac glanced at the lawman. He knew pain and fatigue and frustration had stripped Stever's nerves raw. His own were not in much better shape, he admitted to himself.

"If I start firing," he forced himself to explain patiently, "they'll know we're onto them, and maybe move back to the front without giving us a decent shot. Besides, Tom's out front somewhere. We don't want them moving until he's back safe inside."

"Let Langston take care of himself," Stever retorted without a trace of sympathy. "He was fool enough to go out there on his own!" He bit further words off abruptly as if he regretted what he had already said. Angrily he directed his gaze back through the window.

Isaac watched him for a moment longer, then did the same. What was Tayback planning? he wondered. And what was he waiting for? Isaac sniffed the air again. The scent of smoke seemed stronger now.

A single shot shattered the glass near his head. He ducked by instinct. The shot was a signal. Guns roared from the woods. Bullets snapped overhead, and shards of glass slashed through the air. Isaac could only stand hunched beneath the window. To have lifted his head would've been to take a bullet in it.

The firing dwindled to a halt, and a rebel yell sounded in its aftermath. Isaac swung his carbine up over the windowsill, and saw the riders burst out of the woods. Ragged gunfire thundered from the upper floors, but the riders came on unscathed. The snow was slowing them, but they seemed more accustomed to riding in it than during their earlier charge.

Isaac sighted on the nearest rider and fired. His target toppled sideways from the saddle and sprawled in the snow. Isaac could hear the reports of Stever's Colt. He wondered remotely whether the lawman could really hit anything left-handed. He had no time to keep score.

His thumb crooked reflexively to cock the carbine so he could reload, but he saw the riders were already too close. Calmly he set the rifle aside and pulled the Dragoon Colt from leather. He fired once, but the rider ducked low on his mount at the last moment, and the shot went high. Isaac had the sudden frantic impression that he was moving too slowly and achieving too little.

From the corner of his vision, he glimpsed one of the riders reach the outer wall near Stever's position. The lawman's gun seemed to be empty. The outlaw swerved his horse alongside the wall. He flung himself from the saddle and caught the sill of the window with both hands. For a moment he hung there, legs flailing for purchase. Then he clambered over the sill and fell heavily to the floor inside. He scrambled to his feet, clawing for a belt gun.

The twin blasts of Stever's sawed-off blew him backward off his feet. Stever's cry of agony mingled with the roar of the shotgun. The lawman sank to his knees, clutching at his wounded shoulder. Isaac flashed on his warning to Stever about the shotgun's recoil.

He tried to get off another shot with the Dragoon. More of the riders were at the wall, below the range of fire of the defending rifles on the floors above. Desperately Isaac swung the Colt to bear. Then something that felt like a bolt of lightning crashed into his skull, slamming him mercilessly down into darkness.

Sharon heard the gunfire echoing up from below. She blinked her eyes against the haze of smoke that had gradually permeated the narrow rear corridor where she and Fawn knelt by adjoining windows.

The charge of the outlaws had carried them beneath her range of vision. She had fired at them as they came and had heard the crack of Fawn's rifle as well. She did not think either of them had hit anything.

The smoke stung her eyes and blurred her vision. She knew there was a fire somewhere that would have to be dealt with before it had gone too far. Maybe it was already out of control. But the fire would make no difference to them if they were not able to repulse this latest assault by the outlaws.

She had heard shots below and then a muffled explosion, louder than the other reports. She thought someone had screamed at almost the same time. Then had come another shot, and silence. She believed she could hear men's voices now, raised in raucous tones. She strained her ears, but did not recognize the voices. She rose to her feet.

Fearfully, she glanced around at Fawn. The Indian girl met her gaze with troubled eyes that, she guessed, mirrored her own. She turned her gaze back to the mouth of the corridor. A short passageway led from the stairway to this rear corridor. Anyone entering the corridor from the stairs would have to come down the passageway. Did she see the shadows of men lurking there, or was it only the drifting smoke? She fingered her rifle nervously and smothered a cough.

She sensed movement at her shoulder as Fawn joined her. "I think they are coming," the Indian girl whispered. "They must have gotten inside the building!"

She left unspoken what that obviously meant: the men defending the mission—including Tom—were almost certainly dead.

Sharon shuddered and put the awful thought from her. Her mind could not accept it, and to dwell on that horror would only leave her paralyzed with fear and grief.

Gunfire rumbled from the floor below. A woman screamed. *Sister Ruth?* Sharon thought in horror. A voice bellowed in pain. A man cursed savagely. More gunfire echoed upward. A ricochet shrieked away into silence.

Sharon was conscious of Fawn close beside her. The younger woman was trembling. She crossed herself and leaned even closer to Sharon. She did not seem aware of either action.

The outlaws would be coming now; the certainty of that fact assailed Sharon. Whatever had happened to Sister Mary Agnes and the other nuns below seemed to be over. Sharon realized her mind had frozen into immobility. Vainly she tried to force herself to think.

A shadow moved in the smoke at the end of the hallway. This time she was not imagining it. Fawn gasped. Sharon felt herself stiffening. Booted feet scuffled on the floor, and a man's figure ducked briefly into view from the hallway. Automatically, Sharon flung her rifle up and fired. The roar of the shot merged with a man's curse. The figure ducked hastily from sight.

"You little girls quit playing games," a coarse voice ordered from the passageway.

"Stay back, or I'll shoot!" Sharon found her voice.

The outlaw chuckled from his hiding place. "We already know that, sweetie. But you best not be doing it again. We aim to come get you both, and you can make it hard or easy on yourselves. It's your choice!"

Furiously Sharon levered the rifle and fired another round at the end of the corridor. She had heard of ricochets striking a person around a corner from where the shot was fired.

"Now that wasn't nice at all, gal!" the man's voice shouted. Apparently her dubious strategy hadn't been successful. "Now you done made us real riled. You get ready, because we're coming, and we're coming shooting!"

Men's voices murmured excitedly. Sharon's mind began to work as abruptly as if she'd levered the action on her Winchester. There was no cover in the corridor. They would be sitting targets for the outlaws' guns.

"Get down!" she hissed to Fawn. "Lay flat on your stomach. You can shoot from that position. Do it!"

Fawn flattened herself and aimed her rifle awkwardly down the hallway. She glanced questioningly at Sharon.

Sharon lay down beside her. "Here," she whispered urgently, reaching to adjust the rifle. "Put the butt against your shoulder like this. Slide your hand further down the barrel." Sharon called upon images she had seen in history books of men on the battlefield.

She surveyed the results as Fawn obeyed. Her positioning looked better. Sharon snatched up her own rifle. Any moment now the outlaws would gain the courage to make their attack. Kneeling, she raised the rifle to her shoulder. She had never fired a gun from that position before. Without the windowsill as a prop, the rifle seemed heavy and clumsy. She shifted her grip until the balance felt comfortable. Resolutely she lined the sights with the mouth of the hallway.

"Wait until we have a clear shot," she whispered to Fawn, and saw the other girl nod.

In their low positions, they would, she prayed, be underneath any initial volley fired by the outlaws as they rushed around the corner into the hallway. Her strategy might only work for the first few seconds of the assault, but at least their attackers wouldn't find them easy prey.

She saw the shadow appear again, and sensed the tension that stiffened Fawn's prone form. The next instant the same male figure she had seen before burst into the corridor like a desperado, a six-gun blazing in each hand.

Sharon heard the bullets snap somewhere overhead. Their attacker had positioned himself squarely in front of her sights. She pulled the trigger. Fawn's shot roared simultaneous with her own. The desperado slammed back against the wall and slumped. A second man, close on his heels, sprang to cover with a shrill curse.

Sharon realized her shoulder was aching from the recoil of the rifle. She dared a glance at Fawn, and saw the determination etched in the Indian girl's profile. She tried to focus her eyes back on the mouth of the hallway, but the smoke seemed thicker than ever. Her throat burned as she sucked in the foul air.

There was at least one more outlaw out there; she had vaguely seen him duck back to shelter.

"You killed Hank, you little hussies!" a shrill voice cried, as if in answer to her question. "He was my pard—you hear that? We're coming to get you!"

Sharon gripped her rifle and waited. And prayed.

Tom eased through the window into the main corridor. He crouched, Colt in hand. The hallway was deserted. He could smell the smoke, even see it as a faint haze. He thought of the roof blazing three stories above his head. What must conditions be like on the upper floors?

He padded down the corridor toward the stairs. He had left his Winchester outside the window. Its length made it awkward for indoors work. He would have to rely on the Colt.

He saw the outlaw emerge from the parlor in almost the same instant as the fellow saw him. What the owlhoot had been doing there he had no idea—maybe looking for valuables to loot. But he wheeled toward Tom with the reflexes of a gunhawk, his hand swooping to lift his revolver from leather. Tom snapped his arm out to full length and fired. He fired again as his target fell, still clawing at his gun.

Tom dashed to the door of the parlor, but it was empty. His hands moved with automatic precision to replace the spent loads in the Colt. The gunhawk was not moving. Tom sidestepped him and moved swiftly to the door of the dining hall. He swung around through the doorway, Colt leveled in his fist.

In the first beat of time he saw only the broken windows and the dead body of an outlaw beyond the tables. Then his eye fell on the still form lying beneath one of the windows.

"Isaac!" The name was wrenched from him in a gasp.

He threaded his way between the tables, alert for danger lurking within the large room. But the dining hall seemed deserted. He stood over Isaac, and for an agonizing moment he was afraid to look any closer. Then he saw the slow rise of the chest and felt a surge of relief. The old man was alive.

Tom knelt and examined him. A bullet had creased the grizzled head. Isaac would no doubt carry a scar, but he would likely survive. The invading outlaws had either taken him for dead or had not cared enough to make sure. If Tayback had passed this way, he would've finished the job.

There was nothing Tom could do now to help Isaac, so he straightened up and studied the sprawled body of the outlaw nearby. That looked to be the work of Stever's sawed-off, but there was no sign of the marshal himself.

Tom had spent too long here already, he decided. Plainly the outlaws had breached the mission's defenses and were within its walls. He left the dining hall and mounted the stairs, staying close to the wall, gun at ready.

On the second floor the smoke was worse. He all but stumbled over the lifeless body of an outlaw lying a short way down the corridor.

"Mr. Langston!" Sister Mary Agnes slipped into view from a doorway in the hall.

"Sister! Are you all right?"

She nodded tersely. "When they came up the stairs, we shot this one." She crossed herself as if to punctuate the statement. "Then we retreated to one of the rooms and barricaded ourselves there. They did not pursue us."

That didn't sound like Tayback, Tom thought. "What about—" he began anxiously.

"Miss Easton and Fawn are upstairs," Mary Agnes anticipated his question. "I was coming to check on their safety when I saw you. I believe the remaining outlaws went up there when they left us." Again her hand moved in the sign of the cross.

A mingled series of gunshots reverberated down the stairwell. Then a man's anguished voice could be heard crying something about his pard.

"Stay here!" Tom snapped. He turned and ran for the stairs, bounding up them to jerk himself to a halt near the top.

A twenty-foot passageway led to the rear corridor where Sharon and Fawn probably had positioned themselves, he remembered. He could hear men's voices raised in angry excitement. They seemed to be coming from the short passageway itself. He had no idea how many outlaws were left; he had lost track of the dead during this bloody day.

"We're coming to get you gals, right now!" a man's voice yelled.

Tom sprang to the top of the stairs. He saw the shapes of four men lined up at the far end of the narrow passageway. Their backs were to him. They were intent on the charge they were about to make around the corner into the main hallway.

"Try me first, boys!" Tom barked.

They all pivoted toward him. There was no question of surrender. Their guns came around leveled, but they were all in a row, and they got in one another's way.

Tom shot the foremost one square in the chest. The outlaw lurched backward against the next man, who shoved him aside and fired past his falling body. The shot screamed off stone somewhere behind Tom. The butt of his Colt bucked twice in his fist, and that one, too, was falling. Tom had no time to move or sidestep. He could only stand in the mouth of the passageway and match shots with the desperate men at its end.

He fired again and knew he'd missed the third man. He saw flame lance at him from the outlaw's gun and felt the bullet's heat sear past his side. He fired twice more. The outlaw's gun blasted into the floor as his knees buckled. The fourth and final man lifted his gun to fire. Even though he knew it was useless, Tom thumbed the hammer and pulled the trigger again. The hammer clicked on the empty cartridge beneath.

"You're dead, next!" the outlaw shrieked in triumph.

A powerful arm shoved Tom aside. The blast of the shotgun beside him seemed to shake the passageway. The outlaw bounced off the wall and fell.

"We're even now, Langston," Marshall Breck Stever growled through teeth clenched in pain.

Tom caught his arm to keep him on his feet. He saw the shotgun rigged in the sling of his wounded arm, and marveled that the lawman had been able to fire the weapon at all.

"Sharon!" he yelled. "It's me! Everything's all right! You're safe now!"

She burst from around the corner and reached him in a rush. He wrapped her in his arms. Suddenly—he didn't know how it had happened—he was kissing her and feeling the frantic press of her lips against his. For a moment the smoke and guns and death faded from him.

"Mr. Langston! There is a fire on the roof!" A girl's excited voice dragged him back to the smoke-filled passageway. He realized Fawn and Songbird had joined them. It was the latter girl who had spoken. She had been in the cupola, he recollected. "I have tried to put it out with the snow, but I must have help!" she cried.

"The other students can assist," Mary Agnes stated from the top of the stairs. "Are we safe from the outlaws, gentlemen?"

"Yeah," Stever growled in answer to her. "I been through the whole building. There's no more of them here."

"Very well. I shall have Sister Lenora tend to the wounded with Fawn's assistance. The rest of us will extinguish the fire."

Stever turned to Tom. "Where's Tayback?" he demanded bluntly. "Did you get him?"

"I haven't seen him," Tom said in realization. "Or Segundo, either." He recalled his wonder that Isaac and the nuns had been allowed to live.

"Then they ain't in the building," Stever declared. "This was the last of his men." He indicated the sprawled forms cluttering the passageway.

"I saw him from the roof!" Songbird exclaimed. "Only a few minutes ago, he and the one you call Segundo rode away to the north very fast!" She used her arm to gesture in that direction.

Tom stepped clear of Sharon. He thumbed shells from his gunbelt, and began to reload his Colt as he moved down the passage.

Stever caught his arm and turned him half around. "What are you doing?"

"What do you think?" Tom told him harshly. "I'm going after them!"

CHAPTER 16

THE trail was easy to follow in the snow. It led up into the remote hill country where a pair like Tayback and Segundo could lose themselves from the sight of civilized men. He had not seen them during the actual attack, Tom thought as he rode. Realizing the battle's outcome, they must have turned tail and fled.

"You don't have to do this," Stever had told Tom before he left the mission.

"You ain't in any shape to do it," Tom countered. "Neither is Isaac." He tightened the cinch on Paint's saddle as he spoke.

"You've already done enough," Stever protested gruffly. "Tayback's gang is cut to pieces, and he's on the run."

Tom knew the words must have come hard to the proud lawman. "I can't let the two of them go free." He gestured out the stable door toward the mission. "Not after what they done here."

"Well, then, I'll ride with you," Stever asserted. "I can still sit a horse, by thunder."

"Forget it," Tom told him. "I let him get away once. Now I'll bring him back."

Stever appeared about to argue further, but a woman's voice stopped him. "Tom?"

It was Sharon. She entered the stable and came to him almost hesitantly. Stever turned away, as if embarrassed. He grumbled something under his breath.

"I had to see you before you left." She hesitated, then abruptly stepped forward and gave him a fleeting kiss on his lips. "Come back to me," she whispered.

Tom remembered that parting now. It served to warm him against the bitter cold as he followed the parallel tracks of the two men he pursued. The horses of the two outlaws traveled well together, he noted, as if they were long accustomed to their owners riding side by side.

The miles passed away beneath Paint's hooves. The parallel tracks wound across the hills and through the woodlands. Tom took to cover at times so as not to make an easy target of himself for a bushwhacking. But allowing Paint to walk in the trail already broken by the outlaws' horses conserved the mustang's strength. Tom was unwilling to give up that advantage by constantly keeping to cover. He was counting on the easier going and Paint's wiry endurance to let him overtake his prey.

Fatigue weighed like a burden of logs across his shoulders. The white snow was mesmerizing. More than once he caught himself drifting into a doze in the swaying saddle.

He was fighting off the grogginess as he followed the twin trails beneath a thick stand of trees. Remotely he wondered at Tayback's purpose in entering the woods. The trees would only slow them down. Then his eyes fell on the change in the twin sets of tracks, and the grogginess was swept from him in an instant.

The smaller of the two horses—Segundo's animal—had suddenly shied out and away from its companion as they passed under low-hanging branches. Where the tracks continued ahead, Segundo's horse seemed to be following Tayback's rather than pacing it as before.

Tom saw this and instantly flung himself sideways out of the saddle. He twisted in midair, clawing his six-gun from leather as he fell. He heard the whiplash crack of a shot and had the distorted view of a figure crouched precariously on a limb in the tree above, rifle at shoulder.

He landed flat on his back in the cushioning snow, and snapped a shot up at the figure overhead. There was a cry of pain. Then the rifle fell, and the figure plummeted toward him with a bestial howl. He glimpsed Segundo's cold, fierce face and tried to roll clear. The half-breed's attack was part predator's leap and part wounded man's fall. Tom's snap shot had gone home somewhere, but it had not finished the feral killer. His weight crashed down half atop Tom. The Colt flew from Tom's grip. He floundered desperately in the snow with his opponent.

Then Segundo was on his feet, looming over him. A fighting knife gleamed in his right fist. Tom's fingers scooped up a handful of snow and tightened. He flung the hard compacted mass up into Segundo's face. The half-breed reared back. Tom shoved himself clear and scrambled to his feet.

As he made it, he saw Segundo paw the snow from his eyes and lunge again. A dark stain showed on his coat, and his movements were more awkward than Tom expected. As the half-breed swept the knife around in a gleaming arc, Tom leaned back and let the blade go by. He shot out his right hand and caught Segundo's wrist. He shoved hard to force the knife around in the arc in which it had been traveling. At the same time he bulled in close to the half-breed, wrapping his left arm around him to hug him full into the blade of the knife, now turned inward toward his body. The knife went all the way into Segundo. Tom released his hold and stepped back to let the half-breed collapse on the snow.

Shaken, Tom looked up into the branches of the tree. Only the change in the tracks of the horses had led him to suspect the ambush. When Segundo had scrambled up into the branches from his saddle, his horse had danced sideways in excitement and confusion. Tayback had led the animal on while Segundo gained a perch and crouched in waiting.

Paint stood stolidly fifteen feet away. Tom plodded over to him. Thankfully, Segundo's bullet had not struck the horse.

Tom collected his revolver and mounted once more. A quarter mile from the ambush site he spotted Segundo's horse tied to a tree. Tayback had left his companion's horse there for him and ridden on alone, no doubt expecting Segundo to rejoin him following the ambush.

Surely Tayback had heard the two shots. Did he assume Segundo had been successful in the ambush? Or was he waiting to stage a second bushwhacking attempt?

Tom loosened the reins of Segundo's horse where it was tied. If he did not return for the animal, it would eventually be able to work free. It was the best he could do for the beast.

More cautiously now, he went on. He felt a quickening of his blood and a sharpening of his senses. His prey was almost run to ground.

Paint tossed his head and snorted apprehensively at the same moment as Tom saw the strange object in the snow ahead. He eased Paint forward, squinting in puzzlement. At last he realized what he was seeing. The panting head of a fear-stricken horse was sticking up out of the snow. Tom saw its wildly rolling eyes. He recognized Tayback's big roan.

The animal had all but sunk from sight in a treacherous drift, the likes of which had almost consumed him and his rider once before. The churned snow about him spoke of his futile struggles. A separate trail showed where his rider had scrambled clear of the drift. A set of booted footprints led off into the woods. Tayback had been unable to free the roan, so he had abandoned the animal to die and had kept going on foot.

Tom cast his rope over the roan's head and secured it to a tree. The roan gave a despairing whinny that touched Tom's heart as he continued on his way. He hoped he would be able to come back.

Tayback had set out with a long powerful stride that planted his bootprints deeply in the snow. Tom's mouth quirked when he saw the depth of the prints. Without snowshoes, traveling on foot under these conditions took exhaustive effort. He wondered how long Tayback would last.

Within a mile he was able to detect a shortening of Tayback's stride and a clumsiness to his step. He began to watch the surrounding area carefully for signs of an ambush.

He saw where Tayback had fallen, then picked himself up and slogged on. As he rounded the curve of a hill, he saw the outlaw at last. On a boulder-strewn plain below the hill, Tayback's burly figure moved with the lumbering step of exhaustion. For a moment Tom sat his horse and watched the shambling figure.

"Tayback!" he yelled at last, his voice echoing hollowly.

The outlaw halted, turned slowly to look back. Tom could see that Tayback did not carry a rifle. He must've lost it when his roan went into the drift.

"Come on, cowdog! I'm waiting!" Tayback seemed almost cheerful as he baited him. As Tom watched, Tayback walked slowly to an upthrusting boulder and leaned against it, his arms folded.

Tom rode out across the plain toward him. As he drew near he could see the exhaustion pulling at Tayback's heavy shoulders and deepening the lines of his coarse features. The outlaw's grin was hard around the edges.

Fifteen feet distant Tom pulled to a halt. "You never did learn to watch out for the drifts, did you?" he said.

Tayback shook his head tiredly. "Dang horse went in and couldn't get out. Barely made it clear myself. Had to leave everything behind in that snow."

Tom saw that he had his belt gun. His coat was bunched up to make it easy to draw, but his arms were still folded, and his hands were out of sight.

Tom felt the coldness on his own bare hands. "We missed seeing you at the mission," he drawled. "Not too many of your boys are left."

"A bunch of nuns and schoolgirls shoot my gang to pieces," Tayback groaned. "Who would've believed it?"

"You must've been expecting it, or you wouldn't have stayed clear when things got hot," Tom pointed out.

Tayback grinned ruefully. "Let's say I was being cautious.

At first, I wasn't expecting any kind of defense out of those nuns and the squaws. I figured you and the old slave might give us a fight, but what could you do against all of us? Anyway, when I saw you had them organized, I decided to let my boys go first to see if you had any more surprises waiting inside. I could tell the way it was going when none of my boys came back out. Hated to do it, but me and Segundo lit a shuck out of there. I guessed you'd be coming, if you was able."

"I was able."

"Yeah," Tayback agreed bitterly. "I heard the shots. I guess you finished Segundo too?"

"Just barely."

Tayback's curse had little heat to it. "I'll miss that sorry half-breed. He would've walked through fire for me, you know that?"

"Most likely that's what he's doing now."

Tayback lifted his head to stare up at him. Tom watched his eyes.

After a moment Tayback looked away. "Figured there wasn't no point in me trying to bushwhack you, not if Segundo hadn't managed it. You just won't let go, will you, cowdog?"

Tom didn't answer. He swung a leg over the saddlehorn so he could keep Tayback in full view, and slid from his horse. Tayback watched him without expression.

"Let's go, Tayback."

Tayback shifted a little bit against the boulder where he leaned. "Just what do you want, cowdog?"

"I'm taking you in to stand trial," Tom told him. "I'll have to tie your hands."

Tayback emitted a snort of laughter. "I told you I wasn't going to let you take me prisoner again." He straightened away from the boulder, arms still crossed. "I meant it."

Tom hitched his shoulders. "I figured you did."

Tayback sneered. "You know, I would've bet you couldn't

whip me with your fists, but you did. Well, now I'm betting you can't beat me with that six-gun you're wearing."

Tom no longer felt the cold. A fair fight was out of character for Tayback. And his cross-armed stance was all wrong for a man waiting to draw from the hip. What had Stever said once about Tayback liking a hideout gun?

"It's your bet," Tom said. "Make it."

"Yeah," Tayback growled. His eyes shrunk back into his skull.

Tom didn't wait. He stabbed his hand down for his Colt. He saw Tayback's right hand appear from under his arm gripping the stubby revolver he had held concealed there. Tom's gun was already out, leveled, and cocked.

"Hold it, Tayback!" he snapped.

Tayback froze. The stubby hideout gun was not quite in line with Tom's body.

"You lose your bet," Tom told him coldly. "Drop your gun."

Tayback stared at him from his mean shrunken eyes. Then some of the violence faded from them. "I can't do that, cowdog," he said huskily.

"If you don't, you're dead."

"I reckon I can't let you take me prisoner again. It's like I told you—I might not be able to get loose this time." With the final word he swung the gun across his body to bear on Tom's chest.

Tom fired, and fired again because Tayback's gun was still swinging toward him.

The big outlaw slumped back against the boulder. His gun hand dropped limply to his side. Leaning there, he stared at Tom with hard glassy eyes.

"You shot me, cowdog," he croaked.

"I didn't have any choice," Tom said.

Tayback snorted. "You done got that right!"

His eyes rolled back in his skull, and his gun dropped

from his hand. He pitched forward from the boulder and fell facedown in the snow.

Tom stood there until the cold began to creep into his bones. Tayback never moved. At last Tom checked him, but he already knew Tayback was dead. Tiredly he mounted Paint and headed back to get the roan.

CHAPTER 17

THE morning sun glinted off the snow and cast back reflections like a thousand glittering diamonds scattered across the landscape. Sister Mary Agnes smiled to herself and wondered what had sparked the poetic—even romantic—thought in her mind.

Her eyes strayed to the figures of the young man and woman walking together toward the stable, and she knew the answer. She felt her smile widen slightly. They did make a nice couple.

"It's a beautiful day, Sister." Isaac joined her at her study window. "The snow will be melting right soon now with all this sunshine."

She continued to smile as she looked over at him. "Yes, Isaac, a beautiful day." She gazed back out the window. Tom and Sharon had disappeared into the stable. She made her voice more formal. "Is everything secure?"

"Yes, ma'am." Isaac's tone was still cheerful. "The prisoners are all locked up in the cellar. Sister Lenora's done tended to their wounds. They'll be plenty safe and sound until help arrives. With the snow melting, it won't take long for us to get some assistance in here."

"And how many prisoners are there?"

"Five, ma'am," Isaac told her respectfully.

She had already known the answer, but had asked just the same. Five outlaws left alive, out of about a dozen; she crossed herself reverently. The mission had seen a great deal of death in the past two days. The outlaw chieftan and his men had been rebuked with a vengeance.

"And the fire damage?" she asked aloud.

"I got it patched," Isaac told her. "I'll get after it again this afternoon."

"Very well." She glanced over at him and the white bandage encircling his head. "Don't overdo, Isaac," she cautioned. "Your wound should not be taken lightly."

"Aw, shoot, Sister," he mumbled sheepishly. "Takes more than a little bullet scrape to hurt this old hard head." But she could tell he was pleased by her concern.

Yesterday's fire had been extinguished before extensive damage had been done. She felt a warm surge of thankfulness for the protection that had been granted for her and her flock.

"Where's Langston?" Marshal Stever appeared in the doorway of her study. "Hello, Sister," he added by way of a polite afterthought.

"Tom's out to the stable fixing to ride to Konowa and get the sheriff to come here with some help," Isaac answered his question. "Miss Easton went with him to see him off."

"Is that right?" Stever came into the study and stood with them near the window.

He was looking remarkably well, Mary Agnes noted, although he still moved with care and favored his wounded shoulder.

"You need to see Mr. Langston, Marshal?" she asked.

"Yeah." Stever peered from the window. "I never got the chance to tell him. He may not have realized it, but he's going to be entitled to some hefty reward money for capturing Tayback and some of the gang members." A surprising twinkle showed in his gray eyes. "But seeing as how he's busy, I guess I'll just wait until later to give him the news. I reckon you know, Sister, that you're looking to lose your newest schoolteacher." He grinned engagingly.

Mary Agnes sighed. "I know," she admitted. "I expected it at some point, but hardly this soon."

"Now hold on there," Isaac protested. "I ain't so sure

you've seen the last of Miss Easton doing some teaching here."

"What do you mean, Isaac?" Mary Agnes asked.

"Just a notion I got from some questions Tom was asking me a little earlier."

Mary Agnes stared at him in puzzlement.

"I'll bring the sheriff and enough men to transport the prisoners," Tom said as he turned away from saddling Paint. "I should be back by tomorrow."

"I'll be here," Sharon told him.

He thought there was an almost wistful note to her voice. Her blue eyes were intent on him. He had seen little of her since his exhausted return the night before.

A long night's sleep had revived him. After a hearty breakfast with Isaac, he had made preparations for this trip. Stever was still in no condition to travel, and the authorities needed to be reached as soon as possible to take the prisoners into custody.

"You like it here, don't you?" he said to her now. "I mean you like teaching the Indians and all?"

A faint sadness seemed to dim her blue eyes momentarily. "That's why I came here," she answered quietly. "To teach."

Tom took off his hat. He thought that was probably the right thing to do under the circumstances. "I guess I've been wanting to ask you this almost since that first night in the cabin," he confessed. "I love you, Sharon. I want you to be my wife."

The sadness fled from her eyes. Her face lit up with joy. "I—I thought you weren't going to ask," she said softly. "Of course I'll marry you, Tom."

He reached her in a single stride and wrapped her in his arms.

"I'll be a good wife for you," she murmured against his chest. "It won't be easy to give up the idea of teaching, but I can do it."

"Whoa, there." Tom disentangled himself and held her back at arm's length. "That's what I was fixing to tell you. I been figuring a way so you won't have to quit teaching here."

She stared at him with wide eyes. "What do you mean?"

Tom drew a deep breath. "You know I work for the Bar D Ranch," he began. "Mr. Dayler, the owner, has a standing offer to any of his hands that he'll stake them to a quarter-section of land on his range to get their own place started. He'll hold a mortgage until they can pay him off. It's a good deal. I've thought about taking him up on his offer before, I just never had any real reason to settle down. Now, I guess I do."

"Oh, Tom, that's wonderful!"

"Wait. I ain't finished yet. I did some visiting with Isaac this morning at breakfast. He says there's homestead land still available up in these hills—never been claimed, or else the owners gave it up when things got rough. It's hard to make a go of things in the hill country. I can take Mr. Dayler up on his offer. That'd give us some good pastureland to run a herd on. And then I could stake a claim to a piece of land hereabouts and build our house on it. We'd live there. I could run cattle down on the lowlands, and you'd be close enough to the mission so that you could still get over here to do some teaching. With what they pay you, and what we can make on the herd, I reckon we'll do real fine!"

Her eyes were shining. "I love you, Tom! I'm sure Sister Mary Agnes will agree to my teaching part-time."

"You talk to her while I'm gone, all right?"

She nodded eagerly. "Maybe we can be married here at the mission!"

"I don't see why not," Tom told her.

Then she was laughing and crying all at once, and he pulled her back into his embrace.

"I best get moving," he said when he released her.

She brushed self-consciously at the tears on her face. "Hurry back," she implored.

"Bet on it," Tom said.

His hat was still in his hand. He clamped it on his head. He swung up onto Paint and guided him from the stable. Outside, the sun was warm on his face. A man could find his dreams and live them, after all, he mused as he rode into the hills.

He pulled up once to glance back at the mission. The guns of Sacred Heart were silent.

If you have enjoyed this book and would like to receive details on other Walker Western titles, please write to:

Western Editor
Walker and Company
720 Fifth Avenue
New York, NY 10019